A HUNGER
IN THE
HEART

Kaye Park Hinckley

TUSCANY
PRESS LLC

WELLESLEY, MASSACHUSETTS
www.TuscanyPress.com

Tuscany Press, LLC
Wellesley, Massachusetts
www.TuscanyPress.com

The characters and events in this book are fictitous. Any similarity to real persons, living or dead, is coincidental and not intended by the author.

Publisher's Cataloging-in-Publication Data
(Prepared by The Donohue Group, Inc.)

Hinckley, Kaye Park.
   A hunger in the heart / Kaye Park Hinckley.

    p. ; cm.

   Issued also as an ebook.
   ISBN: 978-1-939627-06-3 (hardcover)
   ISBN: 978-1-939627-07-0 (pbk.)

    1. Families--Florida--Fiction. 2. World War, 1939-1945--Veterans--Florida--Fiction. 3. Desire--Fiction. 4. Hope--Fiction. 5. Florida--Fiction. I. Title.

PS3608.I535 H86 2013
813/.6   2013933877

Printed and bound in the United State of America

10 9 8 7 6 5 4 3 2 1

Text design and layout by Peri Swan.
This book was typeset in Garamond Premier Pro with Shelley Andante Script as a display typeface.

A Hunger
in the
Heart

*To my parents and grandparents
who passed down their stories and their love.
May I feed the hearts of my children,
grandchildren, and readers, with the same.*

1

In the old military Jeep, on their way through Gator Town, Florida's, only traffic light, Coleman's grandfather gave the Piggly Wiggly parking lot a momentary glance that quickly widened to a mad-dog glare. "Aw hell, would you look at that!" C.P. Bridgeman slammed down the brake.

Chief of Police Ed Harper, riding shotgun, bumped his head on the windshield and Coleman Puttnam Bridgeman III, in the back, pitched forward and rammed his face into the split vinyl of the Jeep's front seat. The Chevy behind them squealed tires and the Ford truck following it smacked loudly into the Chevy's bumper. The truck driver barreled out of the cab to find his I LIKE IKE tag crumpled to an irreparable mess.

The truck driver began a litany taking the Lord's name in vain, warning the idiot who put on the brakes that he was going to whip his butt, until he noticed it was Coleman's grandfather who had caused the mishap. He shut his mouth then, and cowered his way back to his truck. Nobody cussed out the mayor of Gator Town to his face.

Coleman's grandfather didn't notice the trucker. He headed into the Piggly Wiggly parking lot like a pit bull raging for a sorry rooster. "Take the boy home!" he hollered to Chief Harper, tossing him the keys to the Jeep. Then he changed his mind. "Hell's bells, come on. I reckon I'm gonna need the chief of police." Chief Harper, rubbing his bruised forehead, trailed Coleman's grandfather into the parking lot.

Coleman's front teeth had cut into his lip and he tasted blood. Through the flesh-colored dust on the windshield of the Jeep, he watched his grandfather and Chief Harper head toward a conglomeration of people in the center of the parking lot. When the crowd parted enough to see, Coleman drew in a sudden gulp of air that closed the sides of his throat and kept him from crying out "Daddy!"

In the middle of the Piggly Wiggly parking lot stood his tall and beautiful father, Putt Bridgeman, bare-chested, beating his shirt against the ground, breaking the air with frenzied phrases that exploded like bullets into the still-gathering crowd. The shadow of a lone live oak in the center of the concrete lot portioned out a softer sunlight to his father's strong arms, splintering into fragments of gold on his father's broad chest, and fingering his father's absent face like Coleman often did when his grandfather wasn't watching. The boy quickly brushed away a tear, although there was no one left in the Jeep to see Coleman cry like a baby.

A half a block away from the Piggly Wiggly, Coleman's mother, Sarah Neal Bridgeman, opened the double wooden doors to St. Michael's Catholic Church to sweep the walkway for tomorrow's Sunday Mass, and she saw the crowds circling in the parking lot down the street. She thought it was a carnival, one of those cheap tours like the one she'd had Fig, the yard man, take Coleman to last year. It was definitely small town, with a peeling merry-go-round and a Ferris wheel nobody could pay her to ride. Except she saw no rides, only people in commotion. Then she saw Putt.

My God! She'd given him his medicine, he was asleep when she left, and Fig was supposed to keep an eye on him. Of course she ought to have known better than to trust a black man with a wooden foot. Once again, Fig's incompetence had allowed her own husband to make a fool of her. Now, Putt was practically naked in front of the whole town.

She ducked back into the church, its altar covered in the white linens she'd ironed, its gold tabernacle between the candlesticks she'd polished, and she felt twice betrayed, by Putt and by God. She stuck the broom in the closet of the vestibule behind the confessional and slammed the door.

Outside, on the sidewalk, she heard voices from the dispersing crowd. "Disgraceful behavior!" one of them said.

"Nobody should blame Putt Bridgeman," reprimanded another. "He's still fightin' the war in his head, poor thing."

"I knew him in high school. He had the best-lookin' body in town."

There was a feminine giggle. "From what I saw today, he still does."

Oh, how she hated their prattle and, worse, their pity. She had the right to blame Putt if she wanted to, and she did. He destroyed her life, and she held him accountable for it. Not one day went by that she didn't recall how he'd chosen saving the life of a Negro soldier over her happiness.

She thought she heard footsteps coming up to the church, so she slipped into the darkness of an empty confessional, but the footsteps passed by. Then she remembered the flask of whiskey hidden in the pocket of her dress. Just touching it gave her a feeling of security. Since Putt came home from the war with a metal plate in his head, she'd depended on the numbing of whiskey as a compromise. But now, leaning against the back wall in this place of reconciliation, she could not come close to reconciling any part of the past decade. The only good thing was Coleman, a child she did not intend and whose father would never again be the man she had married.

She opened the flask and took a long swallow, thinking how Putt had embezzled her happy life, and how God had done nothing to prevent it. Again and again she lifted the flask to her lips, and when she drained the last drop, she took the shortcut home, knowing she'd have to call Dr. Pauly as soon as she got there.

In the Piggly Wiggly parking lot, Coleman's grandfather headed toward his son, who was backed against the trunk of the oak tree. Putt yelled "Stay back, it's a trap!" just as Finias Saylor came out of the store and caught sight of Coleman's father.

"Jesus! Not that pervert again!" old man Saylor bellowed in disgust.

A young woman in a red-and-white polka-dot dress, carrying a bag of groceries with a box of Wheaties sticking out from the top, hurried to catch up with Finias. Together, they followed a group of curious shoppers beginning to circle Coleman's father.

"I told you, Daddy," she panted. "Putt Bridgeman is dangerous."

"He ain't dangerous, Eloise," a man in the crowd shouted as he pushed in front of her. "He's a World War II hero."

Then a meaner voice came from behind: "Yeah, he saved a worthless colored and it's drove him crazy."

At that moment, Coleman's father frantically unzipped his trousers and stepped out of them. "Oh, my Lord! He's fixin' to be naked, right here in broad daylight!" Eloise Saylor gasped, craning her neck to see it happen.

Coleman opened his mouth to call to his father, to warn him

that there were enemies in the crowd, but no sound came out.

"Okay, folks, break it up. Y'all know Putt well enough," Chief Harper said, pushing through the circle to let C.P. reach Putt.

"Put your pants back on!" Coleman's grandfather snapped at his father. When Putt did not, the elder Bridgeman hurriedly took off his jacket and wrapped it around his son. Then with his powerful arm, C.P. forced an exit out of the human chain surrounding the unfortunate spectacle.

Coleman watched their procession toward the Jeep, their twin-like gaits, their long, lean bodies erect as soldiers passing inspection. They might have been marching to the same drummer, the way the father and the son looked just then, but Coleman knew differently. He set his gaze on the single ray of sunlight that passed between their separated heads.

"How long is this gonna go on, Putt?" Coleman's grandfather hissed. His son's response was a confused stare, so the old man shouted his ultimatum. "Hell's bells, I ain't havin' no more bad days. One more's gonna be your last!"

When they reached the Jeep, C.P. put his son in the back beside Coleman, who held out his arms for his father. "Don't baby him," C.P. ordered Coleman, then slumped heavily into his place behind the wheel and hit the dashboard with his fist. "Damn Sarah Neal. What kind of wife can't tell a good day from a bad one? And damn Fig's hide, lettin' Putt get away like this."

Chief Harper stood a short distance from the entrance to the Piggly Wiggly, nodding in empathy with Finias Saylor and his daughter, Eloise. Old man Saylor's words, "repulsive behavior requiring some action from the police," echoed over the parking lot, while Eloise's eyes sought out Coleman's father, an unsettling gaze that the boy translated as certain wickedness.

C.P. hit the horn and the chief came running.

"Reckon Putt's facin' an indecent exposure charge this time," Harper said, flopping his out-of-shape body into the Jeep. "Lucky you know the right person, C.P."

"Hell's bells!" Coleman's grandfather shoved the gearshift into neutral to crank the Jeep. "The boy thought the damn Japs had set him on fire. You'd rip off your britches, too, if you thought you was on fire. Now get out and pick up his clothes, Harper."

"But I got to tell you, C.P.," the chief whined. "Old man Saylor and Eloise back there, they—."

"Can go to Hades!" Coleman's grandfather said, his jaw jutting forward as he stomped on the gas pedal.

The Jeep lurched ahead. Chief Harper let out a yelp and tried to close his door, but his leg hung out and his heavy shoe bumped and dragged over the concrete until they came to a stop beside the pile of clothes.

"Get 'em," Coleman's grandfather commanded. The chief got out, picked up the clothes, and threw them through the window into Coleman's lap.

Coleman's father spoke then. "I couldn't save them," he said quietly.

C.P. Bridgeman twisted toward the backseat. "The devil you couldn't. You saved one too many of 'em already. How many more you got to save?"

As if he'd heard it all too many times, the chief shook his head. "What you gonna do about Sarah Neal's convertible over there? Putt must have drove it down here."

"Well, you drive it back!" C.P. blasted.

Chief Harper scrunched up his fat cheeks so his horn-rimmed glasses mowed into the bush of his eyebrows. He snatched Putt's pants from Coleman's hands, shook them until the keys to the new 1955 Chevrolet Bel Air fell out, and threw the pants back to the boy. "You tell your granddaddy that if he wants to know what he needs to know, he can find me and the convertible at the police station." He headed into the full sun of the parking lot toward the red-and-white car. In the bright light, the chrome bands on the car swirled like liquid mercury, shooting silver rays as if to prevent the chief's approach.

The Jeep lunged forward, grinding under the traffic light, now red, and tearing through the curtain of dust onto the limerock road that led to the inlet and the rambling coquina house that C.P. called the cabin.

Coleman tucked the loose clothes around his father's thighs. His father's dark eyes and his chin strained ahead, but the wind through the window slicked his hair back and flushed his smooth, sorrowful face to rose-violet. His father's hand, the one with the gold wedding band, pressed into the seat beside Coleman's as if to steady his body. The boy touched it gently. His father turned and gave him a welcoming smile, because he'd just noticed his son's presence.

His grandfather twisted in the Jeep as if he'd had a disturbing thought. "Do you know that Saylor woman, Coleman?" His grandfather wore his vicious-possum look where his lips drew back from his teeth, as if he was seconds away from biting, so the boy thought hard about the repercussions of a truthful answer.

"Well? Do you know her or not, boy?" C.P. repeated, turning back to the road. Just ahead was the peeling COME ON BACK TO GATOR TOWN sign.

"No sir," Coleman said, though it wasn't exactly true. He pressed his lips together, and immediately the cut began to bleed again. His father reached over to wipe a finger across Coleman's mouth. He drew in his breath.

Coleman knew, right then, what his father was about to say, and how his grandfather would react to it. "Daddy," he whispered.

"Don't."

His father confessed anyway.

It had been a good day, the first time they saw her. Coleman and his father were squatting on the edge of the inlet, in the middle of the white circle his father had cleared from the scrub so they could play their game of War. With a thorny branch from the scrub, his father traced a fine-lined plan for victory through the sugary grains of sand.

Coleman noticed her first. She was in a bathing suit on the Saylors' dock, watching them. Not like his mother watched them from her distant perch on the porch of the cabin. Different from that. He'd turned away to concentrate on the game he was playing with his father when the woman appeared out of nowhere and stood over them as they knelt in the circle. She disregarded Coleman but seemed very interested in his father. "What do y'all do out here every day?" she asked.

His father stood, dwarfing her, and the woman raised her eyes to his father's face. Coleman could see she was impressed. The corners of her mouth turned up into a pinched smile. "I hear you're a war hero," she said, with a cadence in her voice that reminded him of the old ladies in chunky earrings and bright bracelets and crisp Sunday suits who cupped his chin after Mass on the steps of St. Michael's to call him a precious angel. Except this woman wasn't old, and she didn't wear earrings, but when she stood with the sun behind her, tilting her head to look up at his father, one of her ears glowed blood-red.

His father did not smile, but he put out his hand for Coleman to stand next to him. The woman laughed. She raised a limp wrist to point at their plan in the sand. "What's this?" she asked, studying the coil of lines with her metal-colored eyes, as if his father's strokes in the sand might turn into snakes and bite her.

"It's a battle map," Coleman answered quickly.

The woman eyed his father again. "I heard you took on a whole slew of Japs single-handed just to save some no-account. I declare you must be one strong man." She edged closer.

His father took a step away from her, putting Coleman a little off balance, and the boy stumbled.

"Hey now," the woman said to Coleman, "you're not scared of me, are you? I'm not the enemy." She gave a one-sided smile and ran her fingers through her hair, pulling some of it back behind her blood-red ear.

"No, ma'am, I'm not scared," but his voice trembled.

His father glanced at the cabin as if to make sure it was still there, and then took his son's hand to lead him up the yard, leaving Eloise Saylor standing alone in the cleared white circle. His father looked back once. Coleman looked back, too. She was still there, her eyes bulleted toward them, her hands on her hips, and her elbows like the opened wings of an outsmarted hawk contemplating another chance. She wasn't smiling anymore.

On other good days, when he and his father played War, Coleman noticed Eloise on the Saylor dock again. Occasionally he was aware that his father noticed her too. But the truth, as his father had just told it, seemed of little interest to Coleman's grandfather now. He would be remembering that the chief had something to tell him about the Saylors. He would be conjuring a plan against the sure-to-be-distorted picture a woman like Eloise Saylor could paint of his crazy, unfortunate son. A woman like that, he'd be thinking, sure as hell ought to be stopped in her tracks.

2

Following the Piggly Wiggly exposition and after his father's revelation, the three rode in silence to the cabin. Inside the coquina walls, Coleman's grandfather locked the boy's father away from him again, locked him in the back bedroom to be guarded by Coleman's small, dark-haired mother, whom his grandfather said was crazier than his father—nutty as a fruitcake, in fact—but everyone else in Gator Town said Sarah Neal Bridgeman was pretty as a picture. Coleman would agree.

She was pretty as he watched her through the slight opening of the door: pretty, holding a shaking metal spoon, giving medicine to his daddy, who stared blankly at his wife and wouldn't open his mouth except to say that he was sorry; pretty, when she noticed Coleman and snapped at him to leave; and after he'd gone into the hall to keep close to what was being said and she hollered to him that he ought to know how hard it was for her when his daddy had a bad day, even then she was pretty to him.

His grandfather's words burst from the back bedroom: "This is the last straw, Sarah Neal. If you can't keep your own husband home with his britches on, I reckon I'll have to!"

The old man came stomping down the hall. Coleman pressed against the wallpaper patterned with roses to let him pass, his eyes on the back of his grandfather's green John Deere cap and its gold embroidered letters. B.O.S.S., the letters spelled.

He followed the old man into the kitchen. "Where are you going, Granddaddy?"

"Town. Got some unfinished business with the chief."

Coleman stumbled down the outside steps after him. "Is the chief going to arrest Daddy and send him to jail?"

"He ain't if I say he ain't."

The tinlike smell of his grandfather's sweat swirled around Coleman as he trailed him to the Jeep. Coleman's grandfather motioned to Fig, sitting under the live oak at the end of the drive-way with his wooden foot next to him on the grass. "Put that thing back on quick. You gonna need two feet to drive that damn convertible home."

"Can I go too, Granddaddy?" Coleman asked as Fig started strapping on his foot.

The Jeep lurched backward onto the grass, half on, half off the concrete driveway with the three of them heading down the limerock road to Gator Town.

They stopped in front of the police station, in the place marked MAYOR'S SPOT, to pick up Chief Harper, who insisted, at once, that C.P. zip up the Jeep's canvas top so it wouldn't be obvious to all the rednecks in Gator Town that the head of the police department was prancing around with the part-time mayor, leaving their homes unguarded.

When they reached the Piggly Wiggly parking lot, Fig climbed out and limped toward Sarah Neal's Bel Air. Coleman saw some-thing like envy in the chief's eyes when he watched Fig get into the car his mother had ordered from Gator Town Motors only a few months before. His mother liked to order things, saying she could always send them back if they didn't suit her. But the shiny convertible had suited her. It seemed to suit the chief, too. He moistened his lips watching Fig crank it.

"We could have drove in that one," he said to C.P., his eager eyes on the Bel Air until it disappeared around the corner.

"We could have, but we didn't." C.P. threw the Jeep into reverse and jerked out of his parking place.

"It's got a lot better radio than this old Jeep," the chief said, fiddling with the dials on the square metal box attached between them. "Don't you ever get tired of waitin' for it to warm up?"

"Only thing I'm getting tired of is listenin' to you whine. Ain't nothin' wrong with that radio or this Jeep. Fact is," C.P. said, glancing at the chief with a slick smile, "I mean to be buried in this Jeep, because I never seen a hole either one of us couldn't get out of."

The chief gave a hoarse laugh. "I know that's right. I seen you get out of a lot of heavy stuff," he said. Then he assumed a cautious look, like something was bothering him.

Coleman began to bite his thumbnail. "Are you going to put my daddy in jail?" Coleman asked the chief.

"Course not." But the chief had started to fiddle with the radio again and didn't turn to look at him. Without seeing the chief's eyes, Coleman couldn't be sure if he was telling the truth.

Finally, the radio came on. The boy leaned back on the seat and wrapped his arms around his chest. Beneath the damp left sleeve of his fringed Roy Rogers shirt, he felt his heart pulse out the bass to "What a Friend We Have in Jesus," until his grandfather let out an "umph" and snapped off the radio, just after the words "sins to bear."

"What's the matter, C.P.?" the chief sniggered. "Conscience botherin' you?"

"Hell's bells, if yours don't, why should mine? I ain't the one swore to uphold the law."

"Now when did I not hold up the law, C.P.? Held it up since nineteen forty-aught, so an honest businessman like you could get under it. Fifteen years by my count."

"Those equipment contracts made you and me some money, Harper. But hell, you know I retired from all that phony tourist crap after"—he tilted the bill of his cap in the direction of his grandson—"his daddy got back from the Pacific. I got no interest in sellin' anythin' else to them Yankee twits, or the federal government neither." C.P. tightened his broad hands around the wheel, causing the little black hairs on his fingers to aim dead ahead. "You said you had something to talk to me about, so start talkin'."

"Won't be somethin' you're gonna like, C.P.," the chief said.

A stifling silence took over the Jeep, but Coleman imagined every gear in his grandfather's head grinding, shifting from forward to reverse and back again, trying out all possible directions.

The chief had a twinkle in his eye. He flipped the still-warm radio back on. Up came the finish of "Sweet By and By." Slow as cane syrup, the familiar local voice of the Reverend Bartholomew Throb, host of "Gator Town's Saturday Morning Wake-Up-Call": "Friends, I'm talkin' to y'all out there, dyin' for salvation. Ain't nobody gonna find that sweet by and by if they don't start off the trip right here on Earth. Now, the question is: What y'all gonna do about travelin' today? And the truth is: It ain't the one and only Reverend Bart Throb that's askin' the question. It's Jeee-sus that wants to know! It's Jeee-sus that wants to give you hope."

C.P. clicked off the radio again. "I said get that damn fool out of here!"

The chief grinned. "Better not be talkin' nasty about old Reverend Bart Throb. That'd put a part-time politician like you out of favor in Gator Town."

The Jeep jerked forward, crushing small rocks and acorns

under its wheels, causing white dust to curl over its hood, then part like a curtain opening on the woods ahead. His grandfather was more than irritated now. "This conversation ain't nothin' I got time for, Harper. The boy and me's got things to do." C.P. turned his chin toward the backseat. "Ain't we, boy?"

"Yes sir," Coleman said, but he didn't know what things. He looked out of the window at the thick woods of tall, thin pines and sturdy live oaks lining the limerock road to town. Except for a few open pastures, the woods were everywhere outside Gator Town. Even in the clearings, there were one or two massive live oaks, heavy with Spanish moss to shade the cattle, or a few straight pines towering up somewhere in the middle of land that rolled green or gold, depending on the season. Sometimes on the other side of fallen barbed-wire fences, there were trees of a different sort, not so massive as the oaks, but with leaves tipped in red, strong and straight trees, erect as vigilant soldiers. Coleman loved those trees. What he loved even more was that, though it was autumn and the ground was carpeted with pine straw and leaves, no tree was bare. The safe places were there, beneath the branches, where a boy could hide from a hopeless world when he needed to.

"You want me to say what I got to say with the boy back there?" the chief asked.

"He's ten years old. Ain't a baby no more." C.P. said. Again he half turned to Coleman. "You ain't a baby, are you, boy?"

"No sir." Coleman unwound his arms and leaned forward, cupping his palms over his knees.

"See? He ain't no sniveler," his grandfather said, with some approval of the boy in his voice. "And I told you, Harper, we got stuff to do."

A rusty barbed-wire fence had led them away from Gator Town, like a bony, aging dragon wrapped with a skin of dying leaves. Beyond the dragon was the river, where two men were fishing. Coleman hoped fishing wasn't the thing his grandfather had in mind to do. It was too much of a contest, one Coleman could never win. He might have more luck if they fished on the river, but his grandfather wouldn't fish there. He'd come up in the world. The Bridgemans had their own private inlet, not a piddly river where every Gator Town redneck fished. That was how his grandfather put it, quietly though. After all, the rednecks had elected him their part-time mayor.

The other part of the time, C.P. owned and ran the biggest farm equipment company in north-central Florida. He was the boss of Gator Town, just what his hat said. In fact, the town was nailed and mortared by C.P. He saw that stores, apothecaries, and churches—plenty of churches to feed everyone's soul, except his— were built. If he wanted regular food, he went to the one and only restaurant in town, because he built that too.

Maybe his grandfather remembered that the restaurant was where they were going earlier this morning when they had passed the Piggly Wiggly. Almost every Saturday morning they went there, because his grandfather had a liking for the owner, Imogene Porter. Today, as usual, his grandfather poured on his Old Spice and made sure Coleman dressed in his sissy blue slacks and the new Roy Rogers shirt his mother had given him for his ninth birthday. Before his mother left to clean the church, she had slicked down his hair with Vitalis, in case somebody she knew saw him.

Often, Coleman's father ate with them, but today, even before the Piggly Wiggly incident—in fact, as soon as the sun rose— Coleman knew he would not be going. The day had started off as a bad day for his father.

Now, in the Jeep, Coleman felt the pressing strain of bone through his new sissy blue slacks that his mother said made him look so grown up. Last month she sent Fig to buy them because her baby was growing faster than a weed. She'd told Fig to walk right into Hammett's Department Store like he was as white as anybody else in there and charge at least four pairs of those pants. "Just remind them you work for the mayor, Fig. They won't bat an eye."

His mother had said all that proudly, but nobody except Fig had been listening. Coleman's father was staring blankly at the inlet through the sliding glass door, and Coleman's grandfather was hunched over the white oak table under the three-tiered crystal chandelier, scowling over Sarah Neal's bill from "some travelin' seafood hawker from God knows where," and grumbling about how any woman in her right mind could let herself get talked into ordering fourteen pounds of six-month-old frozen shrimp she couldn't send back.

But Fig had said to Sarah Neal that Coleman was sure enough growing into a fine big boy, and anytime that boy got to needing bigger britches, Miz Sarah Neal could count on him to trot down to Hammett's and get him some, even if it was the white man's store. His mother looked at Fig with appreciation, but his words hadn't changed her opinion of him.

Now his grandfather was saying to the chief, "Coleman ain't a baby, so get on with it, Harper."

The chief began to explain, like he was tiptoeing outside a room he was afraid to enter. "I reckon you know what a bastard old man Saylor is."

"Damn Birmingham lawyer," C.P. interjected. "I'm sorry as hell I ever sold him and his wife that land out there next to my cabin. Tried to outdo everybody in Gator Town, buildin' that prissy pink thing they call a second home."

"Daughter's good-lookin', though," Chief Harper said.

"Nothin' but easy, like her mother was." C.P. raised his eyebrows and poked the chief with his finger. "Years ago, her mother used to sunbathe out on that big pink deck every day at lunchtime, naked as a jaybird. Now the daughter does the same thing."

"Naked too?"

"Just about."

The chief laughed. "Whoo whee, y'all got some neighbors!"

Coleman's grandfather didn't laugh. Instead, he had a faraway look in his eyes. "Emma didn't cotton to naked sunbathin'. Much as she loved the cabin, it's why we moved to town."

"But after Saylor's wife died in that automobile accident, y'all could have moved back out there. Why didn't you?"

"Emma couldn't forget about it, and I got used to eatin' my lunch at Imogene Porter's restaurant, and—hell, never mind, Harper. I ain't cryin' about it now."

"No, it ain't no use, both Emma and Saylor's wife dead. Ain't nothin' to cry about now."

Ahead was the cemetery where Coleman's grandmother Emma Bridgeman was buried. Within a man's length from her marker was the now-flaking sign C.P. erected long ago: VISIT GATOR TOWN. SEE 'EM. FEED 'EM. AND LIVE TO TALK ABOUT IT.

Chief Harper gave C.P. a sly look. "You and Imogene used to be more than friends, didn't you?"

"Ain't out for no gossip session, Harper. You got somethin' to tell me, then do it."

The chief took a breath, leaned as close as he could get to the door on his side of the Jeep, and said, "Saylor and his daughter's fixin' to bring charges against Putt." He was squinting some, like he was afraid of what would come next.

"What kind of charges?" C.P. asked.

Coleman watched the back of his grandfather's head. His grandfather didn't moved a muscle, but the several lines of wrinkles on the back of his neck seemed to close into one deep crevice, and in a fast flash of sunlight, the b.o.s.s. letters on his cap lit up like neon.

The chief spoke again. "Maybe some sort of indecent behavior thing," he said. "I ain't really sure." This time, Coleman could easily see the chief's eyes. He was lying.

"All right," his grandfather said evenly. "What we gonna do about it?"

Chief Harper scratched the inside of his left nostril. "Well, there's one thing we could do, but you won't like it neither."

Coleman realized that the chief cared nothing about his father. Tears came. He couldn't hold them back. "You're not going to put my daddy in jail!"

"No, not jail, Coleman." The chief looked toward C.P., and his eyes shadowed again. "Take me downtown," he muttered from the side of his mouth. "And carry that boy on home, or we'll leave this business unfinished."

Coleman's grandfather spun the Jeep around. Not another word was said, even when the chief got out at the police department and slammed the door.

At the cabin, they pulled in behind the Bel Air. Dr. Pauly's Ford was in front of it. Coleman felt even worse then. He was sure Dr. Pauly was inside the cabin, holding his mother's hand while she mulled over his syrupy words as if they made sense.

When his grandfather climbed out of the car, Fig rose from his usual sitting position under the live oak, his wooden foot already strapped on. "Y'all got it finished up?" he asked, limping onto the paved driveway to meet the boss.

"No, we ain't." C.P. set his eyes on Coleman. "Ain't finished a damn thing because we can't hear ourselves think over his snivelin'."

Fig put an arm around Coleman's slumped shoulders and

squeezed gently.

"Hell's bells, quit treatin' him like a baby," C.P. said, motioning Fig to the side of the cabin, where they could talk quietly. The difference in the color of their faces was indiscernible in the shade of the house, and their voices blended like one long hum.

Finally, his grandfather stepped back into the sunlight and said, "All right, all right. That's enough yappin'. Time to get on back to town." Coleman's grandfather and Fig got into the Jeep and left.

Coleman went into the house and stood outside the bedroom door. His father was lying on the bed, his eyes closed. The light through the partially open Venetian blinds made shadows like bars across his face. His mother and Dr. Pauly stood on either side of his father, arranging a quilt of orange stars. It was a quilt his grandmother Emma had sewn, causing Coleman to miss Mama Nem even more.

When the cover was set, Dr. Pauly took Sarah Neal's hand with something like admiration in his eyes, until he noticed Coleman in the doorway. "Sit with your father awhile. Your mother and I will be on the porch." The doctor's touch on his arm made Coleman cringe.

He didn't like Charles Robert Pauly, mainly because his mother did. She said Charles Robert was one of the few psychologists she'd trust to mess with Putt's mind, and he was "the only man who understood the suffering I'm going through." She said she needed him.

Coleman hated that. He hated the doctor's house calls to the cabin too, and the psychologist's talks with Sarah Neal. He even hated Dr. Pauly's kindness toward his father. He would have to keep an eye on his mother and Dr. Pauly. He couldn't leave them alone for long.

His father was still sleeping, so he left to go into the living room, where he could see the doctor and his mother through the glass doors. His mother was leaning against the stone banister lighting a cigarette. Beyond her spanned the beautifully flowered yard, and beyond that the circle of sand surrounded by thorns and the white beach of the inlet. A sandhill crane methodically waded in the reeds, like a sentinel guarding a sacred place, until it stopped and struck the shallow water with its beak, as if to pierce an invader.

"I don't need a sermon, Charles Robert," Sarah Neal was saying. "It's Fig's fault. If he'd been watching Putt, it wouldn't have happened."

Charles Robert took her hand. "No sermon and nobody's fault."

"Oh yes, it's somebody's fault. But it's not mine. I'm just the one who gets to live with the leftovers."

"And you've done very well, except for—."

"Don't say it!" She snatched her hand from his and stepped back. "Whiskey helps me get through a day. Putt takes the medicine you give him, doesn't he? Well, I take mine."

When Dr. Pauly reached out as if he was going to hug her, Coleman called, "Daddy needs you, Dr. Pauly!"

Charles Robert came inside immediately, and Coleman followed him into the bedroom, where his father sat on the edge of the bed, one hand clutching the sheet, the other covering his eyes. "Where's Sarah Neal?" his father asked.

"Take it easy, Putt," Dr. Pauly said, sitting beside him, touching his shoulder. "She's on the porch."

"I love her," his father said.

"I know," Dr. Pauly said. "I know."

His father began to cry. "The war isn't over for us."

"No," Dr. Pauly answered gently. "Not yet."

The doctor's voice was soft but confident, like the hum of a lullaby. It struck Coleman that it was the same as his mother's voice had once been, whispering goodnight prayers over her son as she knelt by the side of his bed, her hand stroking his. Her voice was real then, and came from some sacred place inside her, not from a bottle of whiskey. He began to ache all over for the return of her gentleness—right here, right now—but his mother was on the porch, and he was left with only a memory, and the desperate hunger to live it again.

3

At the Gator Town Police Department, C.P. told Fig to wait in the Jeep while he went inside. The foolery of the morning bubbled in his head like perking coffee as he made his way down the hall, and pushed open the wooden door with its frosted glass insert that read CHIEF OF POLICE. His abrupt entrance gave Margaret Markle quite a start.

"Miz Margaret, I need to see Harper. Now!" At once, C.P. regretted shouting at the chief's secretary. Margaret was such a gossip. His ill temper would soon be all over town.

"I've never stopped you before," the middle-aged woman answered coolly, continuing to type. "The chief told me what happened this morning. Is Putt okay?"

"Lot of people saw him embarrass himself." He regretted that too, the vulnerability in his voice. He ought to keep more of a distance.

"You know how everybody feels about Putt."

"Yeah. Most of them think he was damn dumb to get himself shot crazy."

"The U.S. Army thought it was worth a silver star. That proves something, doesn't it?"

"Proves the U.S. Army's as crazy as Putt."

C.P. was tired of talking. He moved past her, opening a second door to the chief's inner sanctum, as Harper called it, and went in.

As the door squeaked shut behind him, he heard Margaret dialing the telephone and then "Imogene? He's here, honey, already mad as the devil. God only knows what's gonna happen if the chief tells him what he has in mind. I'll keep you posted, sugar. Bye."

He was sitting when the chief told him. Then he sprang from the chair and kicked it backward. "What do you mean, rape?"

"I tried to warn you this morning, C.P.," the chief said. "Now it's got worse. That little ditty in the parkin' lot won't do nothin' but help her case."

"Her case?" He slammed a fist on the chief's desk. "You ain't gonna bring any case of rape against my boy."

"No, I ain't. But she is. Her daddy lawyer wants her to file a charge with the state of Florida. There might be a trial and—."

"Hell's bells!" C.P.'s knees buckled. He had to pick up the chair and sit down again in order to think a minute. What was he to do? Threaten the Saylors? Pay them off? He was the boss of Gator Town, just what his hat said he was. As mayor, he had to deal with sorry people like the Saylors, agitators who threw things off balance, outsiders who didn't belong in Gator Town. He saw that they were always punished for their brashness, and the rednecks always stood behind him. But now, his own unbalanced son was accused of an act that would stir Gator Town to a fever pitch. If his son was found guilty, he'd never be able to count on the redneck vote again.

Chief Harper was shuffling papers on his desk, mumbling about what ought to be done, but C.P. wasn't listening to him. He was listening to Emma's still-clear voice, a chastening in his head to forget about the politics of the redneck vote and to just believe in his son. Would a man like Putt, who'd given so much of himself to save another, be capable of the violent rape of a woman? Of course not, Emma's voice said.

But Emma didn't live in this world, and really never had. She was much too good to acknowledge its evil. Had she simply closed her eyes, and even her brain, when she challenged him to trust God after Putt was shot crazy? Love is accepting, Emma said. Accepting! He'd never accept the altering of Putt's mind. He'd never accept that his son had been chosen for tragedy, or that his act of heroism had washed away the man Putt was before the war.

He didn't like to think of Putt before the war, when he was strong and smart and happy. It was too painful to remember the little boy Emma gave him to hold in the hospital, wrapped in a worn silk blanket from the Hand-Me-Down store. He couldn't bear to think of the meager birthday parties when he barely scraped up money to buy a gift, or the Pop Warner football games when he couldn't afford to buy Putt a uniform. None of it seemed to make a difference to Putt, as long as his father was at his side. It made a difference to C.P. though. He loved his son, and because of that, he raised himself, and Gator Town, too.

Back then, Gator Town was only an incidental place, hardly more than a pathway suspended from a pitiable U.S. highway near the Suwannee River. The Depression took C.P.'s steady job at a hardware store, so he walked the streets with everybody else, looking for any chance of work. He had a few good days that kept his spirits up, but mostly he was as depressed as the Depression itself. He would never forget that desperate night in the 1930s when he came home jobless again, with only three dollars in his pocket from a week of setting in fence posts for a farmer who was almost as poor as he was. He sat across from his wife and son at an old wooden table to eat four patties of fried corn bread for supper, and he laid the three dollars on the table. Emma looked at the three bills as if they were gold, but didn't reach for them.

"What do I need to do with it?" he'd asked her.

Before she could answer, his little boy touched his cheek. "Use your head, Daddy," ten-year-old Putt had said. The words were a playback of C.P.'s own advice on one of the good days, because words were all he had, then, to give his son. "Always use your head, boy," he'd said. "Hook 'em first! Nobody can nail you to the cross unless you let them."

So C.P. started to use his head, and saw an opportunity. With the three dollars, he bought himself a secondhand suit, and began to hook them first.

Gator Town was ripe for exploitation. Florida's sunny perimeters were being billed to outsiders by some of the state's ambitious offspring, who flashed her wares to rich Yankees wanting tropical getaways and exotic fantasies. But until C.P. used his head and took charge of his own hammer and nails, no one gave a glance to Florida's heart, where Gator Town lay. To change that, he had to have investors, so he poked a threatening finger into the chest of a real-estate agent he knew who had a supply of land and a number of marketable bad habits. All that needed to be done then was to twist the arms of a few bankers with similar secrets, and C.P. had his capital.

Within months, he'd bought cheap land along the U.S. highway and built a string of match-box motels. To offer a little extra, he constructed two or three concrete cavities and filled them with alligators to lure the gullible Yankees who'd formerly bypassed Gator Town on their way to the edge of the state. DISCOVER THE REAL FLORIDA his billboards invited, the words well placed along the clamped teeth of a smiling gator. Carloads stopped to experience the snapping mouths and uncomfortable beds, but only for a one-night stand. Before the sun came up, they left Gator Town as if she were an inexperienced whore mistakenly perceived as worth a detour.

His saving stroke of luck came in 1942, when the U.S. Army fixed its sights on the Suwannee River and pinned a base on the skirts of Gator Town, only a mile from C.P.'s waning motels. He changed the sign to read UNCLE SAM WANTS YOU! and pimped his motels to the U.S. Army, which needed more barracks. A killing was made. C.P. became powerful, Gator Town grew, and hundreds of American boys were groomed for their journey to Europe, the Philippines, the Pacific, wherever the enemy raised its head. The only problem was that one of those boys was his son, Putt. Now, in Harper's office, C.P. ignored Emma's naive voice. He might not be able to fix Putt's head, but he could sure as hell fix the rape charge. He would figure a way to get Putt out of this, whatever it took, just like he always had.

Outside on the street, Fig was waiting for the boss when two young black boys approached the Jeep. He recognized them as two of the boys from Aunt Aggie's. The old half-black, half-Creek woman took in unwanted boys, calling them sons of Jesus, and raised them. Sometimes he wished he'd been raised by Aunt Aggie too rather than by C.P. But back then, things were as they were, and Emma Bridgeman did seem to love him.

Aunt Aggie owned the dilapidated manor house on the edge of Gator Town. The century-old home of a former cotton planter had been deeded to Aggie's mother, a slave of the planter's wife, but Aunt Aggie was the only one of her ten siblings who'd chosen to stay in Gator Town. For years, at C.P.'s suggestion, she'd run the garden as a tourist attraction. She called it the Boneyard, a labyrinth of animal bones, wired and fastened together to form elaborate gateways, arches, and trellises for clinging plants and vines. Everywhere beneath the gateways of bone, flowers rose.

In its time, Aunt Aggie's Boneyard rivaled C.P.'s Gator business. One of her biggest attractions was a parched skeleton slumped on a cedar bench in the sweltering sun beside a trellis of wisteria and honeysuckle. Rumor was that the skeleton used to be her Creek Indian father, whom she readily referred to as "the meanest man I ever knew, before he up and died," but nobody was able to prove it was him. Today, the Boneyard was only memory, but the old woman kept part of it alive and useful. She'd hung the thirsty-looking, bleached-out skeleton in the hallway of the house to remind the boys she took in that "it was Jesus put skin on your bones and gave you water to drink," and if they didn't mind Jesus, they'd "end up scorched as them mean old hangin' bones."

"Hey there, Mr. Fig," one of the boys said, looking at the Jeep. "That's a fine car you got."

"Y'all know whose it is," Fig said.

"Yes sir, but you the one gets to drive it."

"How's Aunt Aggie doin'?" Fig asked.

"Fine," the tallest boy answered, "but she still misses Clayton. She scared one of us gonna turn out like him and end up at the prison farm."

Fig hadn't thought of Clayton Jackson in some time. Most people didn't even know who he was, because he'd lived in Gator Town only a few years. Fig remembered him though. From the day scrawny little Clayton showed up hungry on Aunt Aggie's doorstep at thirteen years old, no amount of food could fill him. "I ain't never seed a hungrier child," Aunt Aggie once told Fig when C.P. had sent him over with the usual monthly eating money of fifteen dollars. "That boy was born empty and I believe he's gonna die that way."

Fig smiled then, not because of Clayton or even Aunt Aggie. He was recalling the fifteen dollars the Boss never failed to send him over with, not even back when business was bad. Fig once asked C.P. why he kept on giving the money for Aggie's boys when he ought to know for a fact there wasn't anybody in Gator Town, except Aunt Aggie and Mama Nem, would give him a vote for it.

The old man had glanced back at him with a funny smile. "Well now, maybe that's why—to keep on the gracious side of two wily women."

Now, the smaller boy tugged at his arm. "Aunt Aggie says Clayton's probably parched-out bone by now because he forgot to work with Jesus."

"Y'all listen to her," Fig said. "Aunt Aggie's fine as they come."

"She says you taught her all she knows about flowers and such, Mr. Fig."

"Did." Everything Mama Nem had taught him.

Suddenly, the window in Chief Harper's office flew open. "Fig, get in here!"

"Uh-oh, you done got in trouble with the mayor, Mr. Fig?" the tall boy asked, running his fingers along the door to the Jeep as Fig got out.

"No, I ain't. But y'all gonna be in it, you touch his Jeep. The mayor's particular."

"We ain't gonna touch it," the other boy said. "Aunt Aggie's teached us manners. Can we just look at it, though?"

Fig started up the steps to the police department. "Go on and look, but you see that window there?"

"You gonna be watchin' us?"

He nodded. "I'll tell Aunt Aggie on you, too."

Fig was grinning when he came into Harper's office, until C.P. said, "You ain't got nothin' to smile about. Saylor woman's gonna bring rape charges against Putt. We got us some work to do."

"Sweet Jesus!" Fig said.

As usual, Harper pointedly ignored him and spoke directly to C.P. "Putt's mornin' show, plus Eloise's babblin' in earshot of everybody—well, it don't look good for him. I know he's a war hero, but nowadays bein' a nice hero ain't what a jury remembers. People like the nasty stuff."

"Then I'll give them nasty. You think of somethin' to keep her from filin' charges, or I'll give them every nasty thing I got on you."

"You do that," Harper warned, "you'll be confessin' yourself."

"Maybe so, but I got plenty of money and plenty of favors to call in. I ought to just cut you loose, find me a bigger gator with some sharper teeth. C'mon, Fig."

"C.P., wait. There might be somethin' we can do. Eloise did say you might want to make it worth her while not to file charges."

"Money? You ain't in on it, are you, Harper?"

"Of course not."

"It ain't like you wouldn't sell your own mother."

"Listen, all I know is Eloise and her daddy's comin' over here at four o'clock tomorrow afternoon, expectin' me to tell them what you're gonna do. And they ain't plannin' to keep the thing a secret unless you pay."

"Do you think I'd actually let that little twerp lawyer blackmail me?"

"Ain't no other way, C.P., except to commit Putt to the state hospital."

C.P. paused. "What would that take?"

Immediately, Fig heard Mama Nem's voice in his head: Stop him! "You don't want to do that, Boss."

C.P. pointed a stiff finger. "You don't tell me what I want to do." He turned back to Harper. "I asked you what it would take."

"Just fill out some papers, but—."

"What kind of papers?"

"Sarah Neal will have to sign. She'll have to say he's crazy."

"Hell's bells, she'd be tellin' the truth, wouldn't she? Get me the damn papers."

The two young black boys were sitting in the front seat of the Jeep when the doors to the police department opened, but they climbed out and scampered down the street before C.P. noticed. The boss didn't say anything as they drove back to the cabin, so Fig calmed himself by talking to Mama Nem. He often did that, conversed back and forth with her in his mind. Just then, Mama Nem was saying, "You know C.P. loves his son too much to send him away, Fig." He nodded, hearing her words. "And you know this, too," she went on. "Mr. C.P. Bridgeman will do nothing unless he has a plan."

He turned to his boss. "You ain't gonna send our boy away. I know you got a plan."

C.P. let out a tired sigh, as if he'd been waiting for Fig to speak. "We got to scrape up everythin' we can on Eloise's daddy, Fig. Let's pay a call on Imogene Porter, she knows more than anybody about that buzzard."

"I knew you wasn't gonna play dead."

"Not unless I have to. But there ain't nothin' I can do to fix his head. Maybe he'd be better off away from here."

"He have some good days."

"Yeah. Some."

Clayton Jackson, sweating in the sun at the prison farm, couldn't remember a good day. Well, maybe one, when he was thirteen and Aunt Aggie said it was time to put some skin on his bones, so she'd dragged him to church to get saved. Heaved from big bosom to big bosom, kissed and coddled, he'd even been given four pieces of sweet bread and some cake at the social afterward, and the preacher said a boy like him, with Jesus on his side, could go any place he wanted to, with one or two exceptions. "Just work with Jesus, son," the preacher said.

But Clayton didn't like to work. He asked the preacher if Jesus could do it all, because he meant to enjoy himself, enlist in the U.S. Army, and see the world as soon as he got away from Aunt Aggie.

The preacher had looked at Clayton like maybe he shouldn't have laid his hands on him in the first place, like maybe he'd take back the saving, but he hadn't. Clayton guessed he was still headed for heaven, even if he was here today, doing prison-farm time for his sins.

Aunt Aggie had been demanding but always big on forgiveness. "Our merciful Jesus came to release sinners from their prisons. And you is sure one of them sinners, Clayton," she said sighing, after he'd stolen two fifty-cent pieces from the poor box at St. Paul's A.M.E. church. She'd taken him to confess and tell the preacher he was sorry. He hadn't been sorry, although it looked like he was, because he cried when he gave back the money.

Aunt Aggie wiped his tears and said they wouldn't mention his stealing again, that she could see Clayton had learned his lesson. He hadn't. Before the next service, he'd taken two dollars, plus fifty cents in change, from the same poor box. He figured Jesus would just keep on saving him no matter what he did. So far, that had proved true. He'd been saved more times than he could remember. One of those times was during the war, and it was a white man who saved him. With all the gunfire whizzing around them, the white man's saving was the only one that sort of took. "I got your back, buddy," the white man had said, dragging him to safety. "I won't let you die." Then, it almost drew him back to Jesus, but it was easy to forget how close to death he'd come.

Now he was here, in this broiling sun, hacking leaves off tobacco plants just because he had to kill a man in self-defense. Still, the food wasn't bad and he had a cot, much as he'd had in the army, or even at Aunt Aggie's. He knew for a fact he'd be saved again. Jesus himself meant for Clayton Jackson to escape this prison.

4

When they got back from the chief's office, Coleman's grandfather left Fig off at the cabin to do some yard work, and then went to Imogene's to see what he could dig up.

"Take the wheelbarrow and get my tools out of the fish house," Fig said to Coleman. "And bring me my bonnet, too." Anytime he worked in the yard, Fig wore Mama Nem's old sunbonnet, kept on a nail in the wall of the fish house.

Coleman smiled. The fish house was exactly where he wanted to go. What he'd found there might be just what he needed to help finish up the business about his daddy. He pushed the wheelbarrow down the long yard until he reached the square stone building on the edge of the inlet where Fig used to live. Fig stayed there only on weekends now, when C.P. came to fish and brought him along to do the yard work. For a while, after Coleman's father returned from the war, and after C.P. gave the cabin to Putt and Sarah Neal, Fig continued to live in the fish house. Then Sarah Neal complained. She told C.P. that Fig's color, the same color as the man Putt saved, bothered her so much that she couldn't get through another day with him living on the property.

Then C.P. moved Fig to his house in town, into a room over the garage, and everyone except Coleman seemed generally happy with that arrangement.

All the yard tools and the fishing equipment were kept in the old fish house. His grandfather's cane poles stood up along the left wall, wrapped around with fishing wire, the hooks taped down with electrical tape. Next to the poles was a table with a hot plate. Next to that was the double rollaway bed, always left open for Fig on the weekends. On the right wall hung a rusty gallon bucket with a lid that imprisoned the night crawlers his grandfather used for bait.

For a moment, Coleman focused his attention on the pine bookcase that held his grandmother's old set of *The Book of Knowledge,* from which she'd read him stories. Just above the bookcase was the carved wooden crucifix with Jesus hanging on it, a twisted figure that reminded Coleman of his daddy.

The crucifix belonged to his mother, but Fig once asked her for it—"Ain't gonna feel bad about askin' her," he said to Coleman one day on their way up to the cabin. "After all, she got one hangin' in every room of her house. Surely she want to share sufferin' Jesus with whoever she can, don't she?"

He'd repeated those same practiced words to Sarah Neal, who stared back at him like she was trying to think up a reason why not, but she couldn't come to one. Finally, she said Fig could have it, because it was small, but she looked sorry she'd given in when Fig put the cross in his pocket.

Now Coleman took the sunbonnet and the shears and put them into the wheelbarrow, along with the hoe and Fig's gloves—tools for the yard—but after this morning, there was one tool he needed for himself. He crawled under the bed to look for the duffel bag. It was right where he'd shoved it, back against the wall so Fig wouldn't find it. The words US ARMY were stamped in black between the buckled straps.

He opened the bag, pulled out the army jacket, and put it on.

Looking at himself in the frameless mirror leaning against the wall, he shoved up one long sleeve to free his hand, ran his fingers across the lapel where there were gold lieutenant bars. He gave his reflection a crisp salute.

Next, he took the newspaper from the bag. He had left it folded with the front page showing. The headline read: "Lieutenant Putt Bridgeman Awarded the Silver Star." He hadn't found a silver star in the bag, but there was a picture of his daddy wearing the same jacket Coleman had on. In the picture, his daddy had a lost look, like he was trying to figure out why his picture was on the front page. Beside his father was his pretty mother. She was looking at his father in the same despairing way she looked at both of them from the porch whenever they played the War game, like she was ready to take any bus back to Cedar Key, where she was from.

Inside the fold of the newspaper was the gun. He pointed it at the mirror, like he had before, but this time, instead of rewrapping it, he set it into the pocket of the army jacket, then pushed the wheelbarrow up the yard.

"You a picture," Fig said when he saw him, "but you gonna get hot in that coat." He took the bonnet from the wheelbarrow and stuck it on his head.

Coleman slipped a hand inside the pocket of the army jacket to touch the gun. The metal felt cold. Should he tell Fig that he'd found it? Maybe he should draw the gun and surprise him. He'd seen Roy Rogers do that in a Saturday matinee when Roy was saving people from the bad men. But Fig had probably never seen Roy Rogers at the picture show. He might even take away the gun.

Nervously, he bit off the tip of his thumbnail and with one short breath between his teeth, he aimed for the rosebush Fig was pruning and blew. The piece of nail flew like a bullet into the glossy leaves, just where he intended it to go. Watching that little piece of himself succeed gave him confidence. "You know what else I found in the fish house, Fig?"

"I know it ain't nice to spit," Fig said. He could have been Mama Nem in the same bonnet, bending and opening the blades of the silver shears at the lowest joint of the rosebush to snap off a branch, except that Mama Nem never made Coleman mad.

"I wasn't spitting." He wanted to get the small business of spitting out of the way. The gun was bigger business than that, but after this morning, what might happen to his daddy was the biggest business, and Fig would know all about it. His grandfather had two fast rules. One, he never let the same mistake happen twice. Two, he always included Fig in his plan to keep whatever happened from happening again.

"Spittin' ain't sanitary." Fig laid a pruned limb across a pile of other dead branches.

"I wasn't spitting. It was a fingernail I bit off."

"It ain't nice to bite your fingernails neither."

The sunlight dancing on Fig's neck reminded Coleman of the candies his mother used to bring him—chocolate kisses, she called them. Maybe he would forget what he'd found in the fish house and fling his arms around Fig, hold on to him like he did when he was small, except Fig would say exactly what Coleman's grandfather would say: "You're too big to be actin' like a baby."

He flattened his back against the fat trunk of the live oak at the end of the driveway. Even through the jacket, he could feel the rough bark of the tree and thought of his father, naked and helpless in the stark morning light of the parking lot, unable to keep from revealing all of himself to everyone who watched. This picture made Coleman want to cry.

Fig put a hand on his shoulder. "Go on and get us some ice water, honey boy, and we'll sit down and drink some together."

He liked when he and Fig sat and drank ice water under the shade of the live oak, but he made no move toward the house to get it, afraid his grandfather would come back before he could pry the ice out of the trays and get Fig to tell him the plan.

Fig eyed him. "You ain't fixin' to cry, are you?"

"I'm too old to cry."

"And gettin' older every day," Fig said.

"One day I'll be older than you. That's what Daddy said."

Fig lifted the brim of the sunbonnet. "Now that's baby talk, one baby talkin' to another. You ain't never gonna be older than me if you live to be a hundred. People born first stay first, unless they get shot in the head like your daddy did in the war. If they don't, can't nobody be older than somebody else if they born after them. You was born after me. I distinctly remember the day."

A smile tugged at the corners of Coleman's mouth. If he wanted to know something, all he had to do was start Fig talking. "Tell me again about when Mama brought me home from the hospital and you were standing right out there by the inlet, and you came running up the yard, much as you could run with your wooden foot, to see what—."

"—Sweet little baby Jesus made for the Bridgemans," Fig finished, stringing the words together, like somebody's long name. "But wasn't just me came running. Your daddy run up faster. He the one had two good feet."

"But Daddy's head wouldn't let him remember I belonged to him. Just you, Fig, just you knew who I was."

Fig raised himself from his knees and gave such a long, heavy breath that Coleman could feel its warmth from over the wheelbarrow. "Yes sir. Fig knew you. He knew you was a little baby then." A slow, impish grin came over his face with the start of the play between them. "And he know you a little baby now."

"I am not a baby!"

"Oh, come on over here," Fig touched Coleman's cheek. "Fig knows there ain't no bigger little boy in the whole wide world than Coleman Puttman Bridgeman III. No sir, Fig knows who you are." Then what Coleman had been waiting for came. "Most of the time, honey boy, your daddy knows too. This morning? That wasn't nothin' he could help. Don't you worry about it. Boss gonna get under it."

Of course the boss would get under it, his grandfather always handled everything. The question was how? Fig stood over him with the answer.

"How's he going to get under it?"

Fig tugged down on the brim of the sunbonnet. "I told you not to worry about it. Now, if you ain't gonna fix us some ice water, take them branches over to the trash pile. Need to burn up some dead stuff."

Coleman felt defeated. He walked over to the pile and scooped up a handful of branches, purposely snagging his thumb with a thorn. "Ow!" he yelled, pretending to be hurt.

"What you gone and done?" Fig grumbled, limping toward him. He rolled up the long arm of the jacket and rubbed his finger into the blood and plucked out the barb. "Go see if Miz Sarah Neal can't find a Band-Aid."

"I don't need a Band-Aid. I'm not a baby," Coleman said stubbornly. "And I'm not crying, either. I'm brave like my daddy was in the war." His attempt to turn the conversation back to his father ended when the sound of grinding gears came up the dirt road and the Jeep rocked into the driveway.

Coming to an abrupt stop, his grandfather glared at the sunbonnet. "You look like a damn-fool woman."

"Whoo-whoo, Mama Nem gonna haunt you," Fig jokingly

warned. "Told me to wear her hat every day I work in her yard. Told it in her will, too. Remember that?"

"You remember who gave you a job to do," Coleman's grandfather said.

"I remember, Boss," Fig said, more serious. "You took a poor little old boy that used to have two good feet and give him a job to do."

"You know that ain't the job I'm talkin' about. There's a bunch of stuff from Imogene in the Jeep, couple of nasty pictures and a paper with Saylor's signature that shows he fixed up a crooked deal. Take it all over to Harper and tell him to show it to Saylor. See if he wants to push on with that damn suit."

"Lord, lord," Fig said. "Miz Imogene keep a library on all her clientele?"

"Just about. Now get on over there." C.P. tossed the Jeep keys to Fig, who caught them with a satisfied grin.

"Can I go with him, Granddaddy?" Coleman stuck a hand in his pocket to feel the gun. "I can help."

His grandfather's eyes set on the jacket Coleman was wearing. In his mind, Coleman heard his grandfather say "Take off that jacket right now and give it to me!" Then he imagined his grandfather finding the gun in its pocket, and hearing him holler, "Hell's bells! Where'd you get this?" But surprisingly, all his grandfather said was, "No, you can't go with him. Pick up them yard tools and take 'em back down to the fish house, boy." He turned to Fig, getting into the Jeep. "Don't turn your back on Harper. He's close enough to the oven to smell the cookies. Just lay out all that junk we got on Saylor. If his daughter don't back down, tell Harper we'll just take care of the business ourselves. Then leave it to me."

"Gonna leave it to you, Boss. What comes to you is best for all of us," Fig said, craning his neck through the Jeep's window. He still had on the sunbonnet.

C.P. snatched off the hat. "Give me that! Want them to think we're all crazy?"

"No sir!" Fig said. "We sure don't want them to think we all crazy. One or two of us is enough." He backed out of the driveway, grinning.

The old man stood staring after the Jeep for a minute or two, his fingers absently caressing the sunbonnet in his hand, then he tossed it to his grandson. "Take that down to the fish house too. I reckon Fig needs it."

"When he gets back, can he stay over and spend the night in the fish house?"

"What's that blood on your hand, boy?"

"A thorn. Can Fig spend the night?"

"A thorn? Next time wear gloves." His grandfather headed for the house, then turned around. "How's your daddy?"

Coleman shrugged. "Mama won't let me in the bedroom."

C.P. rolled his lower jaw a moment. "I got to talk to your mama." He continued into the house, but just before the door slammed shut behind him, he called back, "Get out of that jacket, boy."

Sarah Neal was finishing her Rosary in a chair beside Putt's bed. She made the sign of the cross, then straightened the quilt that covered her sleeping husband's thighs, her fingers lingering, feeling the warmth of his skin through the orange stars, remembering how it used to be.

He touched her hand. "I'm sorry, Sarah Neal."

She snatched her hand away. "Does that make it a good day?"

"No, it's not so good."

"It sure as hell isn't! And you ought to be sorry. You ruined my life."

C.P. appeared in the doorway "Ain't you ever gonna let go of that stuff, woman?"

"You don't know enough to talk about it," she said, not startled at his sudden presence. "You come over here, dump Fig off, say your hello and good-bye, and then go back to town. Even on the good days, you don't stay around unless the fish are biting."

C.P. noticed the rosary beads lying on the bed beside his son. He picked them up and flung them toward her. "Take these on out to the kitchen and say a few prayers while you drain that bottle you've got under the sink."

"Leave her alone, Daddy," Putt said. "It's my fault."

Sarah Neal stood abruptly. "Well, it is certainly not mine," she said, leaving the room, knowing Putt would resist his father's attempt at constraint and follow her.

Putt left the bedroom to go to Sarah Neal. Beside her in the living room, he took her arm. "I know it's not easy for you, but it's like war lives in my head, behind some door that I can't keep from opening no matter how much I try. I love you, Sarah Neal. I'm sorry."

She let him take her in his arms, as if his embrace was all she waited for. Then she pulled away. She'd made the decision. This time she meant to stick to it. She would leave Gator Town to go back home to Cedar Key, and she would tell him, soon.

From the fish house, Coleman could see the distant figures of his mother and father inside the living room, framed by the glass doors like actors on a distant movie screen. Still wearing his father's jacket, he walked up the yard, over the neatly mowed grass, breathing in the sweet smell of Confederate jasmine that Fig had planted along a low fence. He passed the rows of azaleas, hibiscus, and gardenias, all telling of Fig's handiwork, and came into the cabin through the kitchen door.

He found C.P. sitting at the table eating a ham sandwich. His grandfather fixed his eyes on the jacket. "You keep disobeyin' me, boy, I'm gonna have to send you over to Aunt Aggie's for some manners," he said, biting into the bread.

"Is Daddy better?"

"I reckon."

"Are you waiting to talk to Mama?"

His grandfather didn't answer. He got up to open the cabinet and take a bottle of whiskey from Sarah Neal's stash.

"Granddaddy, what do you want to talk to Mama about?"

"None of your beeswax, boy," he said, setting the bottle on the table and taking another bite of his sandwich. "Ain't you gettin' too big for your britches all of a sudden?"

"I can help with the business about Daddy."

His grandfather grinned. "Oh you can, can you?"

"Yes sir, I can."

C.P. wiped the mayonnaise from his mouth with a paper napkin. "How you gonna help? You ain't even dry behind the ears."

"But you said I wasn't a baby."

C.P.'s eyes softened and he reached for the boy. "Come here, son," he said.

Coleman moved into his grandfather's open arm, which was unbearably heavy around his slight shoulder, but he relished the rare closeness to a man he both feared and revered. He was proud to be C.P. Bridgeman's grandson. He wanted his grandfather to be proud of him too. Now, with the gun in his pocket, he could make him proud. Just like Roy Rogers, he could destroy the enemy and make everything right for his mother and father. After all, he practiced War on every good day, down by the inlet. He was able to recognize the face of an enemy.

The first time Eloise Saylor intruded upon them, she said she wasn't the enemy, but she lied. She was as much an enemy as the damn Krauts and Japs, as much an enemy as the man his daddy had saved. The first time Eloise came, his father stepped away from her, but she didn't give up. She came again, like enemies do. She asked his father to her house for lemonade. If he had the gun then, he would have made her stay away from his daddy. He would have shot a hole straight through that pitcher of lemonade she made his daddy drink.

Now the weight of his grandfather's arm intensified, and the furrow between the old man's brows reminded Coleman of his father when he drew plans for their battles.

"Coleman, I know you ain't no baby," his grandfather said, his voice very deep. "That's why I'm talkin' to you like you was a man." He stopped and took a breath. "If your daddy was to have to go away from here, you think you and your mama could handle it?"

Coleman shrugged out of his grandfather's grip. "Go away?"

"There are some things goin' on that might make that happen. I just want to know if I can count on you."

Of course he could be counted on. That was what he wanted, but he did not want his father to leave. "I don't want Daddy to go away."

"Well now, I don't either. I'm tryin' to work on it, but I ain't sure what'll happen, so—."

The sound of the Jeep coming into the driveway caused his grandfather to go to the door. He opened it for Fig. "What did Harper say?"

"He gave me these." Fig held out a set of papers for his boss. "Said Saylor thinks he can beat anythin' you got on him. The chief thinks you ought to pay him off if you don't want a trial."

43

"Dammit!" C.P. slapped the papers against the table.

"What are those papers for, Granddaddy?" Coleman asked.

C.P. ignored him, stuffed the papers in his shirt, and turned to Fig. "Let's get out of here. I got to think." They left to go back to town.

Coleman went into the dining room and saw that his mother and father had gone onto the porch. His mother stood next to the railing, her chin angled toward her feet as if she was trying to see what held her where she was. She looked like a delicate question mark, thin and indecisive, with no answer in sight.

His father's low voice blended with the hum of the crickets starting up. "I adore you, Sarah Neal, you and Coleman," his father was saying. He touched her face.

Something fluttered like wings in Coleman's heart, until his mother twisted from his father's hand. "I can't live in this damn war anymore," she said in her whiskey voice. She pitched her cigarette out into the yard, and for a split second it looked like a tiny star falling.

5

Clayton Jackson squinted in the Florida sun, looking up at the tower. He could see the opaque shape of a guard and the occasional glint of a rifle. Below the tower were two sleeping dogs tied in the shade.

It was too hot to work. Even the dogs knew it. He could take off the long-sleeved infantry shirt, but the insignia of sergeant on his arm was worth a little extra sweat for the notice he got from it.

Lifting his assigned hatchet knife, he whacked off a stalk of tobacco. It slapped to the ground at his feet, so he kicked it aside into the pile of others, gathering up the broad green leaves to lay them out on a platform of sticks for wilting and drying in the sun.

"Hot as hell, ain't it?" he said to Dewayne, the man who slept on the cot next to his in the prison barracks.

"Reckon so, you in them long sleeves," Dewayne answered, looking at the shirt as he dumped his pile of tobacco onto the drying rack. "That thing ain't even yours, is it? Bet you stole it. You wasn't never in the war."

"It's all kinds of wars."

"Smart-ass. If you're so smart, why are you here?"

"Here today, gone tomorrow."

"You gonna break out?" Dewayne indicated the guard in the

tower. "He'll shoot you first, and if he misses, them dogs will trail you. Ain't no safe place to get to."

"Yeah, it is. I got me a safe place."

"Where's that?"

"I got me an old granny. She give me this once." From the shirt pocket, he pulled out a phosphorescent statue and cupped his hands around it. "Look through my fingers. See how she glows in the dark?"

"Well, I'll be damned."

"It's a magic charm to keep me safe. My old granny told me that."

"That ain't no magic charm. That's Jesus's mama."

"It is?"

Dewayne took another look. "Uh-huh. It's Jesus's mama, all right. I seen her before, but she wasn't lit up then. You steal her too?"

"I told you, my granny give her to me for a present. You ain't got to steal a present. Some things is free."

"Yeah, I reckon some things is." He laughed. "But you ain't."

"Well, I'm gonna be," Clayton said, turning his face upward. "Just give me one good day, Jesus, and I'll be outta here, safe and free."

Dewayne laughed again. "Safe and free? Jesus's magic mama's got a lot of work to do." He nodded toward the prison graveyard, past the base of the tower where the wooden crosses marking prisoners who'd tried to escape stuck out of the ground. "Over there's the onliest place on earth somebody like you's gonna find safe and free."

The next morning, Coleman saw his mother lying on the living room sofa, where she had slept last night. She was holding a rosary. He kept watch on his mother's face and saw how the pieces of early sun came through the glass doors and stroked her pale cheeks, touched her closed eyes. He saw how her lashes, wet from crying, quivered as she whispered her prayer, and how her trembling fingers moved from one bead to the next, touching each one gently, as if soothing a baby who was hurt. He prayed too. He prayed the whiskey voice would leave her for good.

Then his mother noticed him and sat up. "Do you think it's a good day?"

Before Coleman could answer her, the telephone rang. She rose, ignoring it, then went down the hall into the bathroom and closed the door.

He went to his own room and opened his closet. The jacket was there, crumpled on the floor where he'd left it the night before, the gun still in its pocket. He put on the jacket and took out the gun, weighing its heaviness in one hand, wondering if his father ever killed anyone with it. When he heard the telephone ring again, he quickly stuffed the gun back into the pocket and headed toward his father's bedroom.

His mother came out of the bathroom. Apparently, she'd decided to answer the phone. As she passed him in the hall, the sweet soap smell of her morning shower hovered around him, and from within it a scent of whiskey. She lifted the telephone receiver and said immediately, "Come over if you have to, C.P., but I don't understand why you won't tell me whatever it is right now."

Coleman cracked open the door and peeped into his father's room. His father lay on top of the intricate old quilt as if sewn into the center of a red-orange sun. "Daddy?" Coleman whispered. "Daddy?" He knew he had to say it several times. If it was a bad day, his daddy wouldn't remember he was a father.

"Hey, son," his father said. It looked like a good day. His father was even smiling.

From the kitchen, Sarah Neal rattled on. "I've given him his medicine, C.P. I don't need your constant reminder."

Coleman eased the bedroom door shut, closing out the sound of his mother's voice. "Can we play War, Daddy?"

His father looked painfully at the jacket Coleman was wearing, and his left eye flickered. "Where's your mother?"

"She's on the phone."

"Hand me my shoes then."

They walked into the hall and waited until Sarah Neal hung up the phone and took a whiskey bottle from beneath the counter. She opened it for a couple of long swallows, put it back, and grabbed a dust rag.

When she went into the living room, they slipped toward the kitchen. Coleman could see her dusting the end table by the sofa. She picked up the small framed wedding picture from its place under the brass lamp and held it to her heart.

"Coleman," she said as if he was standing in front of her. "Did you know your daddy had this picture with him the whole time he was fighting in the Pacific?" His mother often went on like that when she thought no one was listening. "Before he left, I gave your daddy two things: this picture and a little statue of the Blessed Virgin Mary that glowed in the dark. Did you know that, Coleman? He had the picture and the statue with him when he was shot crazy."

Then, as they reached the kitchen door, her voice changed to the one he despised. "And do you know who's responsible for that? The whole damn U.S. Army and one spineless black man who couldn't save himself."

His father drew in a tired breath. Then the door banged shut behind them, and her voice was silenced.

When they got to the inlet, the sand lay exposed, white and

round as a Eucharistic host. Long ago, his father and Fig cleared away the scrub, and then his father devised the game of War to play with Coleman. Only his father knew where the enemy hid, somewhere Coleman never thought to look.

The game was always the same. His father drew an X in the middle of the white circle of sand with a long stick and said, "This is where the enemy is." Then he drew another X, some distance away from the first one. "And this is where we have to go to get away."

But today, Coleman touched the gun in his pocket and asked, "Can't we just kill him?"

"No, he can't be killed, not in the game."

"Because we couldn't play the game if we killed him?"

"Yes, that's right."

"And in the game, he can't kill us either?"

"No. Not in the game. It's not real."

"But it was real when you were there."

"Yes."

"And you killed the enemy."

"Yes."

"But you saved one life."

"I couldn't save the others. So many of them died."

"You saw them die?" His father didn't answer. "Daddy?"

"Yes."

"Did it hurt?"

"Yes."

"But you came home. Mama said if you hadn't come home, if you'd died in the war, I wouldn't even be here."

His father's eyes filled as he pulled his son close. "Then I'm glad I didn't die, Coleman."

There was a wonderful moment of silence when his father

pressed his face against the crown of Coleman's head. "There's something I want to show you," he whispered, "but we'll have to wait until dark."

"What is it?" Coleman looked up at the underneath part of his father's chin, where the sandy-colored stubble of his beard stopped growing. "A present?"

"Yes," his father said. "A present."

Later in the afternoon, during the game, his father lay face-down on the edge of the inlet in the white circle of sand, playing dead. Coleman was the first to notice his mother coming from the porch. He watched her move closer to them, as if somebody's life depended on it. She had on a navy blue dress with a white collar and her dark hair fanned out wildly from the sides of her face, like storm clouds threatening a pale evening sun. Her eyes fell fearfully on his father, who didn't see her, and then on Coleman.

"Daddy's all right," Coleman called out to his mother before she reached them. "It's a good day."

His father got up then. An expression of relief passed over Sarah Neal's face, until her brown eyes narrowed and the skin around them crumpled, as if she was burned up by the thoughts in her head. But his father smiled, looking at his wife like he could eat her with a spoon. She turned from his gaze and reached for Coleman.

"It's not real," Coleman said to her, afraid they would be punished for playing War again.

"Yes it is, Coleman." His mother slid her hand, like silk, down his face. Then she cut her eyes toward his father as if she could see the metal plate inside his head and it was not what she had bargained for.

His father scooped her up, holding her like a baby, and his mother gave a surprising laugh. Then all three of them laughed until some remembrance came over his mother's face. She shoved her palms against his father's chest. "Let me down, Putt," she said.

His father's smile faded, but he kept hold. He bent his face into hers and kissed her.

"Now!" his mother demanded in a determined voice after she'd kissed him back.

His father released her gently. His mother smoothed a wrinkle from her dress.

"I love you, Sarah Neal." His father said the words like a child seeking forgiveness, his fingers stroking her sleeve, but his mother stepped back, as if she'd remembered what kept her from loving him in return. She looked at Coleman.

"Give me that jacket," she said.

He took it off and gave it to her, the gun still hidden in its pocket. He held his breath as she wrapped her arms around the olive-colored material and squeezed it to her breast as if she was trying to love it. "I'm going to punish both of y'all if you don't behave," she warned, her voice trembling a little. Then she walked up the yard.

When she reached the porch steps, she hung the jacket over the railing and sat down in the rocker with her knees pulled to her chest, watching them like she always did, as if she wanted to go back to where she came from.

More than once she had said it: "I'm going back to Cedar Key." If she ever left, Coleman wasn't sure she would take him with her, but he was positive she wouldn't take his father. She would leave his father for Fig to take care of because Fig knew how, but mostly because it would serve Fig right for being who he was.

When C.P. drove up, his mother went inside, leaving the jacket and the gun in its pocket slung over the porch's banister.

His grandfather watched as Coleman's mother gave the nightly sleeping pill to his father. Then he ordered Coleman outside so he and Sarah Neal could talk privately, but when the boy reached the porch, he noticed his father's army jacket, still slung over the banister. He put it on.

Even through the glass, Coleman felt their tension. His grandfather had given some papers to his mother and she was flipping through them. "How could you betray him like this? I won't send him away!" she shouted.

"Sh!" C.P. hissed. "You'll have Putt comin' out here."

"I wish he would. He needs to know what his own father plans to do with him."

"It might help if you'd lock the door when it's a bad day. You never lock the door, day or night."

"My house is not a prison, C.P."

"Your house?"

"All right, it's yours. Everything's yours, including your son." She struck the papers against the dining room table. "And this is what you want to do about him?"

"Somethin's got to be done with him, Sarah Neal."

"Oh, why can't he just be like he was?"

"Hell, it ain't a sweet world. He ain't never gonna be like he was." He pointed to the papers. "That's a place for people like Putt who need looking after."

Sarah Neal thrust out her chin. "It's a place for nuts, and you know it."

"Well, he ain't exactly normal. Most days he's walkin' around crazy, with that metal plate in his head."

"So what do you think they can do for that? Polish it up?"

"Oh hell's bells, I don't know!" His grandfather looked like he was going to give in a little, then the look passed. "There's somethin' else besides Putt bein' crazy." He took a breath. "Eloise Saylor says he raped her."

Coleman tried to read the consequences of his mother's stunned expression as his grandfather went on. "Harper says Eloise's daddy is fixin' to turn the charges over to the state and he don't know if she ain't already told it to the newspaper. Says there's already some reporters snoopin' around askin' questions."

His mother laid a hand over her eyes. The touch of her fingers seemed to drain the color from her face. "Putt would never rape anyone," she said in a meek voice, one that used to evoke sympathy in Coleman, until he learned what came after it.

"Eloise swears he did," C.P. said. "We got to deal with it, Sarah Neal. If we send him away, it might help us all."

"It's not true!" Cornered with reality, his mother threw up her arms like a saint waiting for another sacrificial arrow to the heart.

"You ain't got the picture yet, Sarah Neal. Truth don't have nothin' to do with it. It's whoever squeezes out from under the shoe first. Now sign this." He took a step toward her.

"I won't sign it. If you want to send somebody to the nut house, then send yourself. God knows you'd qualify for it."

Her mention of God was all it took to set him off. "Oh that's right, bring it down to religion. That's your problem, Sarah Neal. You think all you got to do is pray on them beads and somebody's just gonna fly down and save you from misery. Well it ain't gonna happen. Hell, like it or not, Putt's crazy. Can't nobody save you from that."

His mother glared coldly at C.P., then shut her eyes tightly as if she could make the old man and what he'd said disappear. "It's so unfair. And it's all the fault of a sorry man who couldn't save himself. I'd kill him if I could."

From the porch, in the frayed jacket of his father, Coleman heard her words. All at once, the face of his enemy had changed.

Eloise was not his worst foe. His biggest enemy was the man his father had saved. He pulled the gun from his pocket and rushed into the living room. "I'll kill him for you!" he cried, the barrel pointed straight at C.P.

"Good God!" his mother screamed.

"Give me that!" C.P. yelled, grabbing for the boy's wrist.

"No, it's mine. I found it. I want to kill the enemy for you, Mama," he said, sobbing. His mother took the gun.

A strange expression, one he'd never seen before, appeared on his mother's pale face. At first he thought she regretted taking the weapon from him, but then she burst into tears. "See what you've done?" she cried, waving the gun in C.P.'s face.

His grandfather looked astonished. "What I've done? Hell, y'all are crazy as loons." He charged into the kitchen. "I'll handle the thing myself."

"No you won't," his mother said, following him down the steps. "I'll handle it!"

Coleman moved behind her until she stopped in the shadows of the live oak. In the driveway, C.P. climbed into the Jeep, its headlights flipped on like swollen twin moons.

"Get rid of that gun!" his grandfather called as he backed out. "And lock the door to the cabin. You don't ever lock the door. At least try to keep him out of trouble!"

Dust like battle smoke billowed over the hood as the Jeep took off with a screech, heading toward Gator Town.

His mother stood staring until the dust settled, then she reached for Coleman. He could feel the weight of the gun in her hand as it hung over his shoulder. "You never saw your daddy with Eloise Saylor, did you?"

It wasn't that he wanted to lie. It was just that he knew what she wanted to hear.

"No, I never did," he said.

The next morning, Sarah Neal made Putt a breakfast of bacon and eggs. Coleman sat at the table, biting his fingernails, while she searched the cabinet for a tray. "Why can't Daddy eat with us?" he asked.

"It's another bad day. He'll eat in his room."

"Where's Daddy's gun?"

"In a safe place, Coleman. A gun is a dangerous thing, it could accidentally kill somebody." Coleman stood up and went down the hall toward his father's room. "Where are you going? Don't you dare mention War to him!"

"Why can't I play War with Daddy?" he asked, turning toward her. She noticed his eyes, the color of Putt's, with the same vulnerability. She ought to be a better mother to him. "Because it's not a good game for either one of you. Anyway, the war's over."

"It's not over. Daddy says it's not."

"Your daddy's crazy, Coleman."

"No, he isn't crazy. Fig says he isn't."

"Fig. What does he know?"

"He knows who I am."

"What's that supposed to mean?"

"Fig said Jesus made me just for the Bridgemans."

"Well, that's true."

"And Fig says there's a war."

"Oh, I don't know why C.P. keeps that man! The war is over. He ought to send Fig away instead of your daddy."

"You said you wouldn't let him send Daddy away!"

"Of course I won't," she said, but right then she couldn't think of one reason why she shouldn't, except that she loved Coleman, and Coleman loved his father. She wanted to love Putt, too, like he was before, Putt in his uniform at the USO in Cedar Key, where they'd met—his laughing eyes; his tall, taut shape; his teasing way that made her as buoyant and restless as a child awaiting Christmas morning; and their first dance, when he held her like cotton in his arms while Bing Crosby sang from the jukebox "All of me, why not take all of me . . ." Ironically, she found herself thinking Putt actually had taken all of her the moment he offered his life for somebody else.

Coleman was biting his nails even more furiously. She took his hand from his mouth and bent toward him. "You never knew your daddy when he was normal, before what happened in the war mixed up his head." She was going to say that Coleman would have loved him so much more and that her son's happiness had been spoiled too, but Coleman interrupted.

"See, there is a war! Fig says the devil fights a war in our heads against Jesus."

"I've had enough of that. I will not let Fig speak for Jesus!" She pulled Coleman's hand away from his mouth and gave an exhausted sigh. "Do you want your fingers to bleed, Coleman?"

She left the kitchen and went into the living room. Through the glass doors she caught sight of the stark silhouette of a sand-hill crane on the edge of the inlet. It stood motionless against the tangerine sky of morning as if waiting for opportunity, a crayfish or a frog to feed on. She'd seen the crane before. It was always alone. Almost immediately, a cloud eclipsed the sun and the scene darkened. The bird appeared to notice the withdrawal of light. It stretched its long neck upward and gave a series of croaking sounds, as if weeping for the sun's return.

When she went back into the kitchen and saw the disenchanted face of her son, Sarah Neal felt as if she might weep too.

She touched Coleman's chin, lifting it. "When Fig comes, you can go to the fish house and play with him," she said hoarsely. "But no crazy war talk, you hear me? And don't go far. It looks like rain."

6

Coleman sat next to Fig on the rollaway bed, the contents of the duffel bag between them.

"All this stuff under that rollaway and I don't even know it?" Fig said as he fingered the paraphernalia.

"There's more than this. I found a gun under there. A silver gun."

"Go on! Fig'll sleep over a lot of things, but a gun ain't one of 'em. Show it to me."

"Mama took it away."

Fig smiled like he had doubts about the gun. He nodded toward the newspaper Coleman was holding. "What's that paper say?"

"It says my daddy saved a no-account black man."

Fig snatched the paper and squinted at the words. "It don't say that. It says 'life.' Right there, see? 'Hero saves a life.'"

"Uh-huh, but Mama said the life my daddy saved wasn't worth what it cost him. If my daddy hadn't been a hero, things would be like they used to be. Mama and Daddy would be happy."

"Honey boy, a hero makes a choice to put somebody else ahead of his self. Your daddy made that choice. He must have thought it was worth it."

"I wish he hadn't. I wish I had his gun back. I'd shoot the man Daddy saved."

"No, honey boy. You go holdin' the devil's hand, he ain't but an arm's length away from grabbin' your heart."

"But it's not fair!"

"Right now, fair feels far away, but don't go dirtyin' up your sweet fine heart by tryin' to gun it down."

"Why not?"

"Sweet Jesus has somethin' better for you. All you got to do is reach for it."

That night, after she gave his father a second dose of medicine and after she emptied the last bottle of whiskey, his mother kept walking around the house, bumping into things and crying. Coleman asked for the gun, but she wouldn't give it to him. She'd hidden it, she said, in a safe place, and he was never to think of that gun again.

The next day his father slept until noon, and his mother didn't seem to notice when Coleman left with him for the inlet, to resume their game. They played without rest until it grew dark. Then his mother appeared on the porch. It was going to rain, she warned them in a slurred but anxious voice. They had better come inside.

His father ignored her, saying he wanted to show Coleman the present he'd promised.

In the distance, Coleman could see his mother's fingers fly to her mouth as his father led him to the darkest edge of the inlet. Squatting by the water, his father thrust his hand just under the surface, moving it slowly from side to side until dazzling pieces of light like stars burst through his fingers.

Coleman drew in an awed breath.

His father looked pleased. "Now you make them."

Coleman thrust his own hand into the inlet. The same light that bled from his father's hand came through his own and sparkled in infinite patterns between his small fingers, like hundreds of morning stars.

"Where does the light come from?" Coleman asked, stirring the inlet again.

"It's hidden in the water, like hope hides in darkness," his father said, "until somebody reaches for it."

Coleman stood and the stars disappeared, replaced by wide interlocking circles swelling on the surface. There was a loud crack of thunder and a flash of lightning.

"Putt, bring him back!" his mother yelled frantically from the porch.

A second crack of thunder, and his father's hands flew to his ears.

"Daddy, come on. Let's go." Coleman started for the house.

"No!" his father shouted, digging his fingers into Coleman's shoulder. Then his father let go of him and took off toward the fish house.

Coleman looked up the yard for direction, the rain stinging his cheeks. In the blurred light of the porch lamp, he saw his mother immobilized, gripping the railing like she'd never let go. He would have to fight this battle alone, so he ran after his father toward the fish house.

Inside, flashes of lightning splashed over his father's back, coloring him amber, then army green, then amber again. As if he'd known it was there, his father dragged the duffel bag from under the rollaway bed and rummaged through it. "Where is it? Where's the gun?" His father threw the bag across the floor and grabbed Coleman around the shoulders, pushing him toward the door. "It's a damn trap. They're all around us. We've got to get out!"

Coleman squeezed his eyes shut. This was not their usual War. He didn't like this battle.

"Daddy," he cried, trying to wiggle himself loose. "I don't want to play."

Lightning flushed his father's twisted face and the boom of his father's voice exploded over him. "You have to. We can't let them win!"

Coleman was afraid, and a small sound of pain escaped from his lips.

"Jackson! Are you hit? I've got you, buddy." His father scooped him up and carried him quickly to the slip, setting him down gently in the bow of the boat. "I won't let you die."

"Daddy, I'm Coleman!"

"Don't be afraid, Jackson," his father said to nobody Coleman could see. Then, laying a hand on his son, he said, "I'm going to save the others."

An enormous flash turned the fish house to the color of a star. His father rushed inside. "Daddy, come back!" Coleman cried.

His father reappeared with an armload of things from the boathouse and began to throw them into the water. "Sonofabitch! You crazy sonofabitch, you should have saved them!"

The rusty gallon bucket hit the bow of the boat and bounced inside, scattering crawlers. "I should have saved them!" his father yelled.

"Daddy, it's not real. The real war's over," Coleman shouted, but his words went unheard.

The hull banged into the far side of the boathouse as his father climbed in. He said nothing to Coleman, but he cranked the motor and backed out of the slip into the inlet. When they were way out, he turned off the motor. The rain had stopped and his father seemed calmer. He turned to Coleman and quietly asked, "Why did they have to die?"

"For war, Daddy, but it's over now."

"It's not over."

"But you saved a life," Coleman said.

He watched his father take up the almost empty bucket of bait. One by one, he threw the night crawlers into the water. Above his father's head, the moon strained behind the clouds and a few small pools of unstable light showed fish converging around the shell of the boat. Around and around the fish swam, gyrating their bodies as each night crawler fell, making stars as they snapped the crawlers into their mouths. When there was none left, the fish swam away and the water stilled, and his father sat staring silently.

"Daddy?"

"It's all right, Jackson. I'm here." Then he cranked the motor again.

By the time they reached the slip, the sky had begun to churn itself inward and then sprawl out, stretching and burrowing smears of black over the last remnant of moon. When thunder split the air once more, his father yelled, "Grenade! Run!"

At first they hid in the darkness of the fish house, then his father dragged Coleman over the wet grass toward the cabin. They passed Sarah Neal halfway up the yard and she followed them, calling out their names.

They burst into the cabin, his mother trying to hold on to them, but his father shoved her into the corner of the bathroom with Coleman next to her. He left them there, and locked the door from the outside.

His mother's eyes darted anxiously from wall to wall until a look of realization Coleman did not understand crossed her face. "Hail Mary, full of grace," she cried as she yanked on the doorknob. "Help us!"

Abruptly, his father threw open the door and almost fell into the bathroom. His mother was pressed into the corner, holding Coleman next to her.

"Don't cry! Don't make a noise. I'll keep you safe," his father said, crouching and backing his body into theirs.

His mother began to push tiny sounds out of her mouth. She pushed against Putt's back, but he edged in closer, until Coleman's cheek was flat against his father's spine. For a strange moment, he felt secure.

"Putt, please!" his mother cried. "There's no one here but us, Coleman and me."

"The enemy is here," his father said in rasping voice. "We can't let it win."

Coleman's thoughts rammed together. Maybe this was real, maybe the black man or Eloise was somewhere in the cabin. Where had his mother put the gun? He could kill the enemy if he had the gun. He tried to wiggle out of the corner, but his father thrust back an arm to stop him. Then he saw the gun in his father's hand. His mother saw it too, and sucked in a loud breath.

The lights flickered with the thunder, and the house went into total darkness. "Oh God, help me save them." His father's frightened words rolled into Coleman's chest, flat and heavy, like blood swelling inside him. Now he was sure the enemy had sneaked in, had followed them inside their own home. This was a real war and it frightened him, because not even his father knew who would win.

Coleman began to cry, and his father turned to touch his face. "I won't let you die," he said again, smoothing his son's hair with the side of the hand that held the gun.

His mother went into hysterics. She grabbed for the revolver, and when Coleman's father held it from her reach, she beat her fists into him. "You're crazy, Putt," she screamed. "I wish you'd never come home at all!"

His father bolted into the hall, his back against the wallpaper, then the lights flicked on again and Coleman could see his face. There were tears in his father's eyes and the same lost look he'd had in the newspaper picture.

His father slid to the floor. The gun fell from his hand, shining like polished silver on the patterned rug until his mother snatched it up. "Coleman, call your granddaddy, fast!" He ran for the phone.

From the kitchen, he heard the sound of scuffling in the hall, and then in his parents' bedroom his mother's angry voice. Just before the shot rang out, he heard his mother cry: "There's no enemy here that you can't see!"

Coleman set down the receiver, the fracturing sound of the gun still in his head. For a while he couldn't make his legs move. Then, from a place that seemed far away, he heard his mother moan, "Oh Putt, why did you do it?"

By the time his grandfather and Fig were standing at the bedroom door, his mother was sitting cross-legged on the quilt, his daddy's head in her lap. She ran her left hand slowly up and down Putt's face. Dangling off the side of the bed was her right hand, holding the gun.

"I tried to take it away from him," she said to Coleman's grandfather, her voice like a child's.

There was a round black hole in his father's temple, but no blood that Coleman could see.

His grandfather didn't blink, only stared into the room, his hands and fingers twitching as if he had no control over them. He moved to the bed and took his son's wrist. "Dead," he said quietly.

Fig fell to his knees. "Jesus, mercy."

"Jesus, Mary, and Joseph," his mother wailed. "Somebody could have helped."

Coleman couldn't take his eyes off the hole in his father's head. Couldn't they just plug it up like they'd done before? His father couldn't be dead. That would mean that for the first time in the game, the enemy had won. He whimpered, and his grandfather glared at him so hard that he bit the inside of his cheek. The taste of his own blood filled his mouth, soothing him and keeping him quiet.

His mother kept moaning and stroking his father's face, until the fingers of her right hand loosened and the gun dropped to the floor.

Coleman looked at it, the gun glinting silver on the rug. All at once, it came to him. "You killed Daddy!" he shouted.

His mother's voice seemed to echo high above him. "Coleman, I didn't," she cried. "How could I kill your father?"

She held out her arms for him, but Coleman backed into the threshold, pressing his palms flat against the frame to block the passage of any enemy who tried to leave.

"I'll need to call someone," his grandfather said blankly.

"I tried to stop him," his mother said when she saw Coleman's grandfather move toward the door. She hugged the body of his father as if it could make a difference.

C.P. looked at her without an ounce of feeling, then broke through the barricade of Coleman's arms and called Chief Harper.

When the chief came, his mother was still holding his father, looking sorry, looking like she might have been able to do something about it, even looking like she loved him.

She walked alongside the stretcher as they carried his father to the waiting ambulance, talking to him as if he could hear her. "If only you hadn't saved his life, Putt. There was nobody to say you had to do that. Nobody."

Then his mother took on the questions put to her by Chief

Harper, who kept glancing over at Coleman's grandfather, waiting for C.P. to tell him who was at fault.

"I'm not responsible," his mother whined. She faced the chief with both her hands wadded into fists like a small child, caught. "But I'll tell you who's responsible."

"Shut up, Sarah Neal!" his grandfather yelled. "Just shut up!"

Chief Harper looked toward C.P., but the old man turned away. The chief patted Coleman's mother on the shoulder and left to follow the ambulance.

The next morning, there was another headline about Coleman's father in the *Gator Town Reporter:* "War Hero Dies Accidentally by Another Gunshot Wound to the Head."

When his mother saw it, she threw the paper in the trash can under the sink and pulled out a bottle of Early Times. She poured a five-ounce Dixie cup full, drank it, and poured another one. After that, it was like she had crawled into the bottle and meant to stay.

7

"Bury him from St. Michael's, and I want the casket closed," Sarah Neal ordered C.P., poking his arm with the fingers that held her cigarette. "Closed. Do you hear me? I can't stand the thought of all those Piggly Wiggly biddies, with their ain't-it-so-sad eyes looking at Putt like he was some kind of freak show." She took another swallow from her Dixie cup. "Those hens have seen more than enough of him already."

The funeral was not held at St. Michael's. Instead it was held in the only mortuary in town, Dove's, because Coleman's grandfather wouldn't set foot inside a Catholic church. He drove them there in the blue-and-white Roadmaster Buick he'd bought Sarah Neal for her twenty-eighth birthday, but it wasn't the car she had wanted so she'd told C.P. to drive it and had ordered herself the Bel Air. C.P. drove them to Dove's without an explanation, and Coleman's mother was silent when they pulled up in front of the building. By then, any idea of what she'd intended seemed to have drowned in her head.

C.P. yanked her out of the Buick as if she was an oversized rag doll, then led them all—Coleman and his mother and Fig—into the place that housed Putt's body.

"Mama wanted St. Michael's," Coleman whispered to Fig.

"Well, at least it looks like a home," Fig said, and gave the boy's hand a gentle squeeze.

Except for the sign in the sloped front yard that had a white bird painted on it, the mortuary looked like any other tall white house with a wide veranda and columns. Just below the painted bird, the sign read DOVE FUNERAL HOME. Underneath that, in slanted letters, *"You will be well pleased."*

Earlier that morning it had rained again, though nothing like the storm the night of Putt's death. Now the sun was out, warm on Coleman's back, making him feel guilty because his daddy would never feel the sun again. On either side of the walk, the grass was a luminous green, like Emerald City in *The Wizard of Oz,* a movie his daddy had taken him to see. He told himself that he shouldn't feel guilty, he wasn't the one who killed his daddy. Still, Coleman thought, he should never have let his mother have the gun. And he should never have left the hall to go call his grandfather. And he should never, ever, have played War with his daddy on a bad day, which was what that day had turned out to be.

Just as C.P. and Sarah Neal stepped up onto the veranda, Imogene Porter threw open the door. "C.P., honey, this is just awful, simply awful." Her lips were pursed like the tied end of a pink balloon when she turned to Sarah Neal. "Sweetie, I'm just so sorry. Putt was such a . . . a good-looking man. I know you'll miss him, sugar."

C.P. put a hand on the sleeve of Mrs. Porter's black crepe funeral dress. "Appreciate it, Imogene," he said, and her eyes filled with tears that looked real.

"Y'all come on in," Imogene said, ushering them through the door as if it was her house. She patted Coleman's shoulder. "Poor little old thing."

Sarah Neal swayed into C.P.'s chest, blowing her sour breath into his face. "One of these days, you're going to have to turn off that old woman's burner."

Fig sat on the back bench, but the three of them—his mother, his grandfather, and Coleman—sat up front. Coleman was squeezed between his mother and his grandfather, his thighs touching theirs. His grandfather wore a suit. Coleman had never seen him wear one before. It was gray with thin, light-colored stripes. He had on a blue tie with a black bass painted on the front of it, just below the knot, and he kept pushing out his lower jaw as if his neck was being pinched in the collar of his shirt. Once, he accidentally bumped Coleman's thigh with his hand as he was straightening out his pant leg. He gave Coleman a quick pat, then he returned to his jaw work.

His mother wore a large black hat with a net hanging off the front. He couldn't make out her face, so he stared at her hands. They were long, thin, and so pale that he could see the delicate bones underneath her flesh. Beside and over and around the bones, tiny veins held her blood. He remembered the silky feel of her fingers when she stroked his face at the inlet, and he imagined that she might touch his cheek again, but if she did, he told himself, he would slap her hand away.

She didn't touch him, though. Instead, she pressed her hands together tightly, her fingers pointing toward the middle of the curtained wall in the front of the room, where there was a large cross. There was no dead body hanging on that cross. The only dead body was his daddy's, closed in the coffin and covered with an American flag.

"At least you saw to it that the casket was closed, C.P." his mother said, her words smacking heavy as thick paint on a canvas.

"You had a point about the biddies," his grandfather said through his teeth, giving a nod to the bunch of women sitting behind them. Each head nodded back at him, like an orchestrated line of hens pecking for food. His mother looked like she wanted to smile at his grandfather, and his grandfather almost looked like he wanted to smile back.

Coleman turned to look for Fig just as Eloise Saylor came into Dove's. Fig rose from a bench in the back and stood in the aisle in front of her.

"Get out of my way," Eloise said, and the hens turned their bobbing heads to Eloise and Fig. "I said move!" she ordered Fig. She had her hands on her hips, and a red purse hanging halfway down her thigh was strung around one of her arms. "This is a free country, isn't it?"

"No ma'am, I ain't noticed if it is," Fig said, not budging.

The woman set her jaw. "If you don't get out of my way, I'll call the police."

Fig set his jaw too. He lifted his chin, indicating to where Chief Harper was sitting. "There's the police," he said. "Call him."

Eloise shifted on her shiny black high-heeled shoes. "Look, I just want to pay my respects."

The hens clucked the name "Eloise Saylor" up and down the pew.

Fig gave Eloise a sweet smile. "Yes ma'am, but I believe your respects has already been paid for, ain't they?"

Eloise Saylor looked at him like she'd string him up if she had a rope. She turned indignantly and clicked across the wooden floor into the vestibule. Fig smiled on hearing the bang of the door. When he got the chance, Fig liked being the boss.

The one and only Reverend Bart Throb stood at the head of the box that held Coleman's daddy. Coleman noticed what he was sure his mother would notice: The preacher he'd heard on the radio was not very neatly dressed for a funeral. His shirttail had come out from under his belt, sticking out on either side of his yellow tie, and there was some dirt under the nail of his index finger on the hand that held up the Bible.

"The Lord has taken Putt Bridgeman, a wounded hero, a suf-ferin' servant of the Lord," Reverend Throb said.

The bones in his mother's hands seemed to rise against the tiny veins. "Damn the suffering heroes," she muttered.

Reverend Throb cleared his throat, looking above Sarah Neal to the ceiling of the mortuary. "Now, we all know that Putt was wounded," he went on. "And of course he was different from the rest of us. But at one time, let us not forget, he was the same as us."

Sarah Neal jabbed C.P.'s knee with a finger. "My God, where'd you find him?"

The preacher cleared his throat again and fiddled with his tie. "Then Putt Bridgeman put his own life on the line."

"His life and mine," Sarah Neal said, like she was giving the response in a litany. The necks of the hens stretched out, and their wide, round eyes were aimed in the direction of his mother.

Reverend Throb's eyes aimed at her too, then narrowed to slits as if he wasn't used to dealing with an audience he could see. "But our hearts are satisfied that Putt is now at peace."

"Satisified? My heart is not satisfied," Coleman's mother said, and the whispering cackles of the hens grew louder, like static on a radio.

Reverend Throb threw up his hands, his index fingers point-ing to the ceiling, and began to spew out words like buckshot. "Today, Putt Bridgeman is free from his burdens. He has been brought back to life. Putt Bridgeman is now fully alive!"

Brought back to life? Fully alive? That was all Coleman needed to hear. His father might be in that box, but he wasn't really dead. He just couldn't get out with the lid closed like that. The boy felt himself being pulled toward the casket as if he were two people, one on the outside and one on the inside of his own body. One of them watched his hands grab the flag and throw it to the floor. The other shouted "I won't let you die," exactly what his father had said on that awful night.

When he tried to raise the lid of his father's box, his mother's voice in the background called for him to come back and sit down, but he paid no notice to her shrieking. He shoved his body against the box, yanking on the locked lid until the box shifted. A spray of red roses on top fell and shattered, splattering crimson blooms and splashing water on the wine-colored carpet.

Then Coleman felt a pinching under his arms and a lifting of himself. When he looked into Fig's anguished face, he cried without trying to stop. Coleman Puttman Bridgeman III cried like a baby.

Naturally, his grandfather ushered all of them out. They passed the black eyes of the hens, crossed the wooden floor of the vestibule, and went down the steps to the luminous green grass, where C.P. corralled them into the Roadmaster. Then his grandfather spun around to face Coleman. "Hell's bells, boy!" A spray of spit landed on Coleman's cheek. "Don't ever fall for that lie again. Ain't nobody can bring the dead back to life."

In the backseat, Fig bent close to his ear. "Nobody but Jesus, honey boy," he whispered.

There was some talk between his granddaddy and his mother about whether Coleman should be allowed to go to the cemetery, but the cemetery is where they all ended up because his mother could make no decisions and Coleman had stopped crying long enough to say he was sorry.

C.P. drove by the graveyard three times before he stopped the car. Nobody was there on the first two passes, but on the last approach, they could hear Imogene Porter's twanging voice as she belted out "America the Beautiful."

When they took their places near the casket, re-covered with the American flag, Mrs. Porter was singing loudly: "America,

America, God mend thine every flaw." She hesitated a little, pressing her lips inward as if her front teeth were trying to escape her mouth, then went on, "Confirm thy soul in self-control, thy liberty in law!"

Coleman's mother turned toward his grandfather in slow-motion rage. "This is not a funeral. This is the Fourth of July. Do something, C.P., or I will."

Four soldiers in formal military attire with rifles stood at attention on the far side of the casket, ready for a gun salute. "Never mind the gunfire," Coleman's grandfather said to one of them. "Just get him down there quick."

"That's up to the preacher," the soldier replied.

Reverend Throb stood in front of his father's box, under the large green canvas tent, sweating and wiping his brow with a rumpled white handkerchief. Coleman's grandfather knocked over a folding chair to get to him just as Imogene, who had finished her solo, was getting ready to sit in it. He tried to catch her before she fell, but she grabbed on to one of the poles and the tent began to sway as she dropped with a major plop to the ground.

"Preacher, say your amens and get this thing over with!" C.P. yelped, panting.

Reverend Throb let out an exhausted breath and nodded toward the flag. "Fold it up, boys." He opened the Bible and read, "Like dust we came. Like dust we go," then smacked it shut with a bang. "Amen."

The soldiers came toward Coleman's mother with the flag folded into a triangle. They tried to give it to her, but she wrapped her arms around her chest and stuck out her chin. "Give it back to the U.S. Army," she said.

"Take it, dammit!" C.P. growled.

"I will not take it," Sarah Neal said. "Save it for the man who put the first hole in Putt's head."

"Hell's bells," C.P. grabbed for the flag. "I'll take it."

Sarah Neal reached for it. "No you won't," she said, her voice dripping with irony. "I'll give it to Eloise Saylor."

Coleman rose between them. "I want Daddy's flag."

His mother gave it to him, and he ran his fingers across the patch of dark blue holding the stars.

At sunset, Coleman went back to the cemetery with Fig. Fig said he had unfinished business to take care of. He wanted to be sure Putt was planted right.

Coleman sat on the ground beside a rusted cross with a circle of plastic flowers, watching Fig limp around the perimeter of the new grave, tapping the dirt with his wooden foot.

"Does Daddy still have his metal plate in heaven?"

"No, honey boy. God took it away by now."

"Why didn't God take it away before?"

Fig stopped tapping. "Maybe you and me ought to plant us a rosebush over your daddy, it bein' his birthday in a new place."

"Why, Fig? God could have made him well here, but He didn't."

Fig flicked a piece of red dirt from the ruffles on the white cross and eased down beside Coleman. "Honey boy, I knowed a sweet white lady, back some years ago, and heard her say to a hurtin' little boy she was holdin': 'Child, just because you got one of your feet cut off, that don't mean God don't want you to get to where you're goin'. The devil might have tried to keep you from travelin', but God's got your name on the trip.'"

"I don't understand, Fig."

"I ain't surprised. That little boy didn't understand neither. He say to that sweet white lady, 'Mama Nem, don't God know it better to take a trip on two feet?' And that sweet white lady say, 'Fig, God see that most people with feet's too busy worryin' over their shoes to care much about where they goin'. But you knows where you goin,' and you gonna have a special wood foot to take you there. Be just like a ticket that's got "heaven" printed right on it.'"

"Did Daddy have a ticket?"

"Yes sir, made out of metal. But by now he done turned it in at the gate."

The day after the funeral, he and Fig planted the rosebush. It had one white bud, petal-tipped in red.

Through the branches, back-lit by the moon, Clayton could see the guard tower in the distance and hear the sound of the barking dogs coming closer. He raised his eyes to heaven to bargain with Jesus.

"Remember how you saved me once? Okay, okay. So I fell out of your boat and got sent up the river again. You don't want me to spend another ten years in that prison, do you?" Then he remembered the statue and felt for it in his pocket. "See here? I got your mama. I'm gonna take care of her too, if you just come on, Jesus' and save me."

The hounds were in his view now, ahead of two armed guards. They burst through a thicket, straining on their leashes, two of them with their tongues hanging out. Clayton quickly ducked behind some thick scrub and scared a rabbit which immediately bounded in front of the dogs. They yapped wildly and twisted their restraints.

"These is some vicious animals, ain't they?" one guard asked the other. "Trained them myself. Ain't no reason to use that government money they give me to send them to a hound-dog school."

"Shoot fire, ain't it the truth! What they gonna do with them dogs anyway, teach them to read?" He let his dog loose from the leash. "Sic that rabbit, boy!" The dog plopped on its haunches, attacking only its tail for fleas.

"I reckon he's tired," the first guard said. "Well, we ain't after rabbits noway." He let his dog off the leash. "Go get him, Tiger!" The hound took off in the direction of the hedge of scrub. "Whoo-whee," he exclaimed. "That one's good." He took out a cigarette and lit it.

Tiger sniffed at the bush Clayton was hiding behind, but neither guard noticed. Clayton could hear them talking. "I just ain't in the mood to find that jailbird tonight," one of them said.

"Me neither. What's one more or less? Unless we trip over him, I say leave him to the devil. He ain't got no place else to go."

Tiger stuck his nose through the scrub and saw Clayton. The dog barked once, but Clayton scratched him behind the ears until the hound began to lick his fingers.

A guard, only a few feet from where Clayton was hiding, called into the dark, "Tiger! Get the hell over here!" The dog backed out of the scrub and ran obediently toward him.

"Damn, ain't I a trainer! You see that old boy mind me?" he said, patting Tiger.

The other guard put both dogs back on the leash. "He ain't around here or Tiger would of found him. He's a smart old dog."

"Why don't you just open up a dog school, the way you trains them so good?

"Might just do that."

Clayton lifted up his eyes to thank Jesus for saving him one more time. There was no doubt he had another new life just ahead of him.

8

After his daddy died, Coleman eventually took up fishing with his grandfather for his grandfather's pleasure, but it wasn't a pleasure a boy could brag about. C.P. liked to keep a running count of how many fish each of them caught. Already this spring, the spring of Coleman's fifteenth year, he had caught one hundred and two more crappies than Coleman. Tonight at dusk, the only time C.P. would fish, Coleman had a chance to catch up.

"Takin' the boy crappie fishin'," C.P. told Sarah Neal as she took three supper plates from the cabinet. Coleman could see the whiskey bottle waiting for her behind the plates. By now she'd moved it from under the sink into plain view.

She raised her heavy lids enough to let in a little light and, one by one, clanked the dinner plates onto the table. "I hope you and the whole U.S. Army are happy over what you've done to me."

Coleman and his grandfather had finally learned to ignore her poor-me attitude, but tonight she was wallowing in it, as if reciting a dull book she'd memorized years ago. She said she wished C.P. and the U.S. Army could have it all on a silver platter to see how they liked it, them sending her back a hero husband with a blown-out head plugged up with metal, all the way from the Pacific to Florida, and nothing else working except that thing that made Coleman. She said they could have that thing on a silver platter, too, for all the sorrow it had caused her.

Coleman's grandfather gave a disgusted grunt and shoved open the kitchen door. Coleman followed him down the slope of the yard toward the inlet, with his mother hollering to C.P. from behind the screen: "Don't you try to make my baby like Putt. He's my blood. Mine!"

Coleman thought maybe he ought to yell something back about her blood being nothing he ever asked for, but instead he climbed into the boat with his grandfather.

When they were some distance out on the water, the old man turned to look back at the cabin. "Woman, you might have had a gripe once," he said as if Sarah Neal could hear, "but now it ain't nothin' but an excuse for drownin' yourself."

After more than a half hour, neither Coleman nor C.P. had caught one crappie. "It ain't the place," his grandfather said flatly. Like Coleman's mother, he was never known to place blame on himself. He wiped a little sweat from under his nose and yanked in his pole over Coleman's head. The line looped above them, but Coleman, seeing it coming, dodged the hook.

C.P. made his way to the back of the boat, ignoring that he'd knocked Coleman over the head with the butt of his pole. He flopped in front of the tilted-up 25 Mercury motor and let it down, his weight causing the dark water to slap up against the boat, a frenzied spray that baptized the place where Coleman's father used to sit.

"If it ain't the place, it ain't the place you stay," his grandfather said. "Bring it in, boy."

Coleman grabbed the rope and pulled in the anchor. The twine cut through his army-green reflection in the water. He wondered how many possibilities they were leaving behind. Of course, his grandfather never worried about repercussions. C.P.'s quick fix was always to find something better a little farther out.

Coleman wanted to get the whole thing over with. "It'll be night soon," he said, because he knew the old man wouldn't fish in the dark. His grandfather liked fishing at dusk, when there was just enough light to see the shadows and just enough darkness to hide in.

"It ain't dark yet," C.P. snapped. "Right now we got a distinct advantage in the fine line between light and dark. It messes up them fishes' minds. It blinds them, puts them off balance. Hell, they'll bite any hook they bump into, then you got them." He cranked the motor again, then steered into the wind.

As usual, Coleman shut out his grandfather's advice. As far as he was concerned, if a fish was damn dumb enough to mess around a hook, it was damn dumb enough to get caught. They were well into the fine line, heading along the deepest perimeter of the inlet.

C.P. fixed on the contest at hand, his lips parted and showing his bottom teeth a little ahead of the top ones, as if every fraction of his body was in competition with another. The wet air blew against his face as they moved over the water, widening his nostrils as he breathed. Coleman imagined the fine-lined air flowing into his grandfather, searching around in his head for his brain, then, like some invisible snake, wrapping around that rocklike organ to strangle it until C.P. admitted the truth about himself: He was as off balance and blind as any hooked fish.

The sun was blood red and had sunk halfway down the black tree line of the inlet. Its crimson rays spilled wildly into the sky and spurted sporadically through the branches. To the right of the sun, his grandfather throttled down. In the distance was the Saylors' dock. Beyond it, a girl and a man were getting out of a station wagon. Coleman kept his eyes on the girl. His grandfather didn't seem to notice them at all.

Farther right, across the patch of flowering briars, was the cabin with Sarah Neal inside. Coleman pictured her standing by the stove, sipping her whiskey from a Dixie cup. She would probably refill it two or three times while she fried bacon into which she would throw shredded cabbage and call it supper. Every other night, when Dr. Pauly didn't come to visit, she would fill up the cup. Dr. Pauly was not expected tonight, so Coleman was sure his mother would be well into the bottle by now. She'd have changed into the powder pink silk Japanese kimono that Dr. Pauly had given her after his return from a conference in Nagasaki, where he'd asked the Japanese how they liked the bomb. She would have nothing on underneath the powder pink silk Japanese kimono except the chain around her neck from which hung both a crucifix and the silver star Coleman's daddy was awarded for "ruining my life" as she put it.

That was what his mother said whenever she caught him looking. Then she'd tightly pull together the two sides of the pink kimono.

She hung the chain around her neck the day after his daddy's funeral, and Coleman thought she sometimes intentionally let it show inside the V-neck of the robe just so she could say the medal was to remind them both that Coleman's crazy daddy cared more for a gutless black man than he did for any of them. She never mentioned what the crucifix was to remind them of, but after she'd swallowed most of the contents of the Early Times bottle, she would look as if she was the one pinned to the cross.

The crucifix irritated Coleman as much as her drinking. When he was younger, he had been awed by the symbol his mother hung in every room of the cabin, awed at the idea that someone would give up his own life, in such suffering, for people who were sinners. His mother had even admitted she was a sinner, yet she wrapped herself in crucifixes, hung them all over the cabin.

And always, she wanted more. Usually she ordered them, but

once, when he was younger, a Christian bookstore had opened in Gator Town. She wanted to see its merchandise and took Coleman with her.

Going through the section of crosses, while Coleman tried to hide between the counter displays, she hadn't been able to find one with the body of Jesus hanging on it. She asked the manager about this, and he told her most people prefer to think not of the suffering Jesus, but of the risen Jesus. "The plain cross," he said, giving her a saccharine smile, "is a symbol of His love."

His mother appeared stunned. She told the manager she was sure most people would prefer not to think of the suffering Jesus, but she never noticed anyone who hadn't experienced pain. Then she got right up in his face: "Love isn't a symbol. It's an irritant, and it'll cost you some skin!" She'd snatched Coleman by the collar and left the store with him.

He hid the feeling, but he was proud of her spunk. Now at fifteen, he thought it was foolish to hang love with suffering. He pitied her. Sometimes he would have so much pity that he would come full circle and pray for God to take away her misery.

He always came to his senses, though, thoroughly angry with himself for such stupidity. After his mother shot his father—and he was not entirely sure she had—he thought she deserved to suffer. If she wanted to wear that cross on a chain around her neck forever, let her. If she wanted to drape the cabin with crucifixes like a hypocrite trying for sainthood, so be it; but she was certainly no saint, and despite what Fig would say, not even God could make her one.

C.P. cut off the motor. The lines on his face scrunched in the wind like the legs of a pricked spider, and pieces of his hair blew wildly from beneath the John Deere cap. "This is the place where we gonna catch 'em," he said, so sure of himself. "Throw out that anchor, and don't scare the fish doin' it."

Coleman eased down the anchor—a rock wrapped around and around with a rope. On the shore, he could see the space his father had cleared for their game. It was a smaller space now, more like a broken circle. Fig wouldn't go near it after Coleman's father died, so the boundary of prickly scrub bushes had thickened until they appeared as stocky armored soldiers guarding a place of reverence. Even at dusk, the broken circle lay bright as the host at Mass.

His grandfather seemed to pay no notice to the circle. "Bait up, boy!" he bellowed, reaching into the bucket for a crawler for himself.

"Hell, why should I? You'll always win." Using *hell* made Coleman feel like a man.

"Watch your cussin', boy. Your mama's blamin' me for enough already." His grandfather stuck the hook several times through the wriggling crawler. "Look here, you have to be sure the bait's on tight so's the fish'll swallow it whole. It ain't on tight, the fish wins instead of you."

"What do I win, a dead fish?"

"See, that's why they don't bite for you." C.P. threw out his line. "You ain't never learned how to play the game. Them fish has got you nailed, boy. Think like that, you'll never catch 'em."

"When I fished with my daddy, we—."

"I'm talkin' about real fishin', boy. Your daddy didn't know squat about that, even before he lost half his mind. Too much like his own mama. Neither one of them could set a hook."

Coleman tried to think of some words to use as a weapon in defense of the two people he had loved most, but he was tired of the battle. Even his cane pole seemed too heavy.

"Dadgasted, that's a big one!" C.P. pulled in a crappie as broad as his palm. The fish flopped around on the bottom of the boat until he stepped on it and grabbed it with a towel so it wouldn't fin him when he took the hook from its mouth.

"Let me tell you, boy, fish is like people. All you got to do is wiggle the right bait in front of them and they'll bite it. People's dumb like that, so take advantage of it." He strung a heavy cord through the mouth of the crappie, pulling it through its gills, then rebaited and threw out his line. "Watch this, boy. I'll show you I know my business." Immediately, he pulled in another fish. "See there? Easy as takin' candy from a baby when you're in the right place."

Oh, how his grandfather irritated him! Couldn't he beat him at least once? He reached for a crawler. His grandfather seemed amused. "Hell, you ain't gonna catch nothin'. Them fish has got you pegged."

Coleman jabbed the hook through the worm and threw out his line. The cork lay on the surface of the water, floating undisturbed.

"Yes sirree," C.P. said. "They got you pegged, ain't they, boy?"

Silently, Coleman ordered the cork: Go under!

"Ain't they, boy?" C.P. asked harshly, waiting for an acknowledgment.

A constant orange ray from the setting sun reflected off the inlet and stung Coleman's eyes, turning him again toward the white space his father had made. His whole body seemed to fly up and into the broken circle, placing itself at its center, spinning itself around and around like a sightless boy feeling for somebody he'd lost in a crowd. The flush of rage that had been growing inside him for years burst into words.

"Yeah, Granddaddy, they got me pegged," he said with as

much bitterness as he could muster. "Pegged with the likes of you."

His grandfather looked at him, dumbfounded. "Ain't nobody said you had to come out here, have they? Anybody ever said that? I'm tryin' to show you a thing or two about fishin,' boy."

"You're trying to show me how much better you are than me. Okay, so you're better. You can beat me, and tonight you can show Mother how you beat me again."

"Don't you sass me, boy. You think your mother cares? She don't care. I'm all you got in this world."

The truth of his words ripped like a hook into Coleman. Even C.P. appeared startled, as if he had unwittingly released a reality he now had to deal with. He let his chin drop a little. "Coleman—." He hung on the name for several seconds, like he was trying to complete a thought but couldn't come to it. When he finally spoke, it was not in his tough B.O.S.S. voice. It was a cautious voice, as if somebody else was the boss and wouldn't like what he was going to say. "It just ain't a sweet world, boy, but don't let it get to you. Hook into 'em first, else the one you least expect will end up lickin' your bones."

C.P. made a move toward him, and Coleman half-expected his grandfather to touch his shoulder, but the old man seemed to catch himself and returned to the contest of fishing.

When Coleman yanked out his first crappie, he saw that the hook was embedded in the fish's left eye instead of its mouth, and when he held the fish in his hand to pull out the hook, it finned him in his palm. There was some satisfaction in his grandfather's eyes as C.P. handed him the fishing towel to wipe off the blood.

Ahead of them, the lights started to come on at the Saylors' cabin. His grandfather noticed and missed the dunk of his cork because he kept glancing over that way. "Hell's bells, lost that sucker."

Carried crisply across the inlet were voices, one of them a young girl's. His grandfather's explanation was that some stranger had rented the place for the summer. He said it like that was the only possibility that would be to their advantage. Or maybe it was old man Saylor's son—he had a son, too. That was the second-best advantage. And maybe the son had a child, which would account for the girl's voice. But what if it was Eloise Saylor, come back? Hell's bells, he knew what Sarah Neal would have to say about them apples!

There was a tug on Coleman's line. He set the hook with a yank and pulled in another crappie. It was hooked in the mouth, where it should have been. By the time night came upon them, Coleman had caught one crappie more than his grandfather. He'd finally won, a small miracle that required some comment, but C.P. started the motor as if he hadn't kept count.

They passed very close to the Saylors' dock, and Coleman looked for the girl. When he didn't see her, a different kind of lack, some absence he hadn't felt before, rose inside him. She was just a girl, though. She meant nothing to him. Then she appeared, small, thin, and about his age. She was carrying luggage so heavy that it bent her forward. For a split second, her face seemed separated from the rest of her, caught in a final ray of sun. It was a pretty face, slowly succumbing to the shadows until he could no longer see it.

C.P. steered into the slip beside the fish house, and they clambered out to tie up the boat. Through the open window of the stone building, Coleman saw Fig lying on the rolled-down bed, his footless limb crossed over one knee. He was turning pages in a volume of *The Book of Knowledge* and listening to a radio news broadcast.

"Ten Negroes who took over the lunch counter at Little

Joe Salvo's Breadbasket Café in downtown Tallahassee today were arrested and taken to the Leon County Jail, where their Washington-based lawyer, Warren Hardy, posted bond. Hardy told officials that his clients would be back at Little Joe's Breadbasket tomorrow. He said the Negroes had every right to eat a ham sandwich in Salvo's place of business whenever they were hungry for one. Hardy also called on all Negroes around Tallahassee who are hungry for freedom to come to the Breadbasket and break Little Joe's bread together."

C.P. gave a grunt and stuck his head through the window. "Don't you even think about it."

"No sir, boss. I ain't gonna think. Y'all give me plenty of broke bread, right here in Gator Town."

When they reached the cabin, his mother was sitting at the table with a cigarette, blowing smoke over the main course of bacon and cabbage. Coleman dropped his stringer of blank-eyed fish into the kitchen sink. His grandfather threw his on top of Coleman's and went to the table to sit next to Sarah Neal.

"Good God Almighty, Sarah Neal," he grumbled, looking at the plate of cabbage. "This stuff again? Ain't we ever gonna have somethin' else?"

"You get what you deserve, C.P.," she said thickly.

Coleman stood by the sink and watched his mother. She had one elbow on the table and was trying to keep her chin cupped in her hand. He wanted her to notice his line of fish, but she was looking at his grandfather, her chin continually slipping out of her grasp, until she knocked over her Dixie cup. His grandfather let out a groan and wiped up the mess with his napkin.

"I beat Grandadddy," Coleman said finally. In the fish-filled sink, some of the live crappie gyrated over the bodies of the dead ones as if they could swim without water.

His mother uncoiled her chin and aimed it toward him, but her eyes didn't follow immediately. She had the vacant look of someone trying to remember a name. This was his mother's second reaction when she was drinking, the quieter one.

"I'm one up on him," he said, hoping for her approval. She didn't give it. She said nothing.

"I told you she don't care. You think she cares, but she don't." His grandfather rose abruptly, scraping his chair across the floor. He walked a circle around the table, then sat again.

His mother's small body seemed to shrink. "I do care," she said slowly. "I'm proud of the fish." She said the word *fish* like it had two syllables and hung on to the end of the last one as if it was her final breath. Still, she didn't get up to look.

Coleman left the fish in the sink, clicking against each other like overwound clocks, and took his place at the opposite end of the table. He noticed that his mother had tried to set it. She had put out a fork, four plates, and two napkins. In the center of the table were three pale roses in a slender green vase. One of the roses bent over C.P.'s plate. His grandfather picked up the single fork and began to serve himself. When he reached for the salt, he knocked the rose into the bowl of crumpled cabbage and bacon and left it for Sarah Neal to retrieve.

Coleman's feelings for his mother softened. It was nice of her to put flowers on the table. She could be nice at times. He found himself attempting to see the cross that hung around her neck, but it was buried beneath the silk of her robe, and he could see only the chain. When he thought of the mess of dumb fish lying in the sink, unseen and unappreciated, he hardened his thoughts until he practically hated her again.

"Some man's in the Saylors' cabin," C.P. said between chews.

Sarah Neal turned with interest, flicked an ash onto her plate, and attempted to focus on C.P. "Well, old man Saylor died last winter, so it isn't him, unless he's been raised from hell."

"It may be his son," C.P. said. "He had a boy that wouldn't have nothin' to do with him, and there's a girl over there, too. Probably here for the summer."

His mother's eyes sharpened. "Is it Eloise?"

"It ain't her, Sarah Neal."

"Well, if it is," his mother said as if suddenly sober, "you know I'd kill her."

Coleman's grandfather grabbed his plate from the table and slapped it into the sink on top of the pile of barely quivering fish. His mother studied a fallen petal as if she'd said nothing out of the ordinary.

The words sat heavy in Coleman's head: Kill Eloise? Kill her, like she killed my daddy? Then the kitchen was as silent as a grave until his grandfather stomped out, the sound of his voice flying angrily back through the screen door as he hollered down to the fish house. "C'mon, Fig, we're goin' home!"

9

After he made it from the prison farm to Tallahassee, Clayton had been so thankful to Jesus for his freedom that he promised, again, to change his life. But it was only the first of many promises he hadn't kept. He'd lied, he'd stolen, once he'd even raped a woman. He was never caught for any of it, because all he had to do was promise again and Jesus would save him, one more time.

The last few months, he worked steadily at Little Joe Salvo's Breadbasket Café. He liked it there. Sometimes Little Joe even let him fry the eggs, although he mostly cleaned the place. But he thought he might stay and honestly reform himself. Then, last week, Little Joe went out of business, and Clayton was out of a job. He thought Jesus was telling him it was time to visit Aunt Aggie.

When he approached the dilapidated house, he noticed a new sign: AUNT AGGIE, PALM READER. She was rocking in the moonlight of the porch, smoking a pipe, watching him come through the yard. "I told you to git more than ten years ago," she said when he came closer.

"I'm changed, Granny."

"I got eyes to see you ain't."

"Any dinner left? I'm starving."

She gave a huff, but rose and opened the door for him. Struck by the air from outside, the hands of the skeleton hanging in the hall moved backward and then forward, as if to brush him away.

The house was still filled with religious statues, the walls decorated as he remembered with dried bones, feathers, and Indian paraphernalia. And the jars were there, too, on the same shelf as before, each one filled with a preserved body organ. His favorite was always the heart, but now there was no reddish color to it. It was completely gray.

In a corner, several black boys slept on pallets, Aunt Aggie's present flock of discarded children. High above them hung a picture of Aggie when she was young. Clayton remembered the picture. He remembered that Aggie had been beautiful. In fact, he'd never seen such a beautiful woman. Even if he could remember the face of the mother who'd forced him out, she wouldn't have compared to the half-Cherokee woman who accepted him at once, the dark angel who took his breath.

In the picture, her hair was in braids and coal black, like her eyes. She was not smiling in the photograph, but sullen. Oddly, he'd never noticed the blurred shape some distance behind her. Now he saw the image of what looked like a white man in a cap. He recalled the prattle of some of the older boys, who said she'd had a honky lover before she got saved. He would have asked Aunt Aggie who her lover had been, then and there, if he hadn't been so hungry.

He went to the table and sat down, knowing she would feed him. Two decks of tarot cards were stacked neatly in the middle of an animal-skin tablecloth, but he moved them aside when she brought him his food. "Always did love scrambled eggs and brains," he said, gobbling them up.

She sat across from him as he wiped his fingers around the plate. He was hoping she'd give him more.

"Ain't no more, hungry man," she said as if she'd read his mind. "And you ain't stayin' here neither. You're blind, dumb, and mean, too."

"Then I'll go find me another place to stay."

"No you won't. Ain't no place on earth for a ruined man the likes of you."

He leaned across the table. "Now Granny, you know you still love me."

She started to touch his face, then gave a huff. Standing, she snatched his plate off the table.

"Aw, sit back down, Granny. Read me my cards. Tell me what you see."

"Don't need no cards. What I see's a hungry boy raised on Jesus. And I hear him tell his granny how Jesus ain't enough, then I see him stealin' all his granny's money and takin' off. Now I see him back, wantin' his granny to feed him again."

All she said was true. He raised his eyebrows and gave her a hopeful grin. "'I once was lost, but now I'm found.'"

"Well, you is found empty. You done ate my food. You done turned down Jesus and cut up your soul." She pulled a long knife off the shelf and pointed it at him. "Git on down the road before I cut out your heart, too."

He was stunned. Was Jesus turning against him?

It was near dawn when he found the circular patch of briars and tall scrub. In the middle of it was white sand, just right for burrowing. There were a couple of lit-up houses on either side. He was still hungry and thought about going to one of the houses to ask for food, but decided against it. He'd wait until the lights went off and hope for an unlocked door. He made a pillow from his shirt on the edge of the circle, under an overgrown shrub, and dozed off, lulled by the gently rolling sound of an inlet.

The day after the fishing trip with his grandfather, Coleman saw the girl again. She jumped from behind the red-tip hedges into the middle of the dirt road, holding a kitten. If he hadn't slammed the brake on his bike, he'd have run over both her and the damn cat for sure. As it was, he skidded and fell off in front of her.

"I didn't mean to scare you," she said, and held out a hand to help him up.

"You didn't scare me." He was embarrassed, and shoved her hand away so forcefully that she dropped the animal. It scampered into the bushes.

"Now look what you've done," the girl said, heading toward the red-tip hedge.

"Hey, I'm sorry," he called to her. "You surprised me. You shouldn't have jumped out like that." But she had disappeared into the thick foliage.

He straddled his bike to take off, but he didn't. He wondered if he should help her, or if she would come back at all. He wanted her to come back.

All at once, with the captured cat in her arms, she emerged from the shrubbery and came toward him. "Her little heart is beating like a drum," the girl said as she stroked the striped kitten.

"I said I was sorry." His voice was too stern. He hadn't intended that.

"It's okay. I have her now." She held the kitten to her face, rubbing her cheek against its fur. "You don't like surprises, do you?"

"Only if I know they're coming."

"But that wouldn't be a surprise, would it?" She was more than pretty. She was prettier than the prettiest girl at school, the one who called him "the crazy man's son." He'd pushed that girl and spent three weeks cleaning gum off the desks at school because of it. But this girl would probably call him the same if she knew about his father.

"Do you want to see the rest of the kittens?" she asked.

"No, I don't like cats." As soon as he said it, he wished he hadn't.

The girl acted as if she hadn't heard him. "There are seven white kittens and this gray-striped one. Where she came from is anybody's guess." She gave a sparkling laugh. The sound of it seemed to say to him that there was nothing at all wrong in her world. It was a sound he coveted, a sound that brought out in him something close to anger.

"I told you, I don't like cats," he said, and started off on his bike. He didn't know why he began to ride. He didn't really want to leave. When he was a good way down the road, he twisted to look back. She was still standing there, watching him. He felt a strange excitement inside, something like a pinwheel of firecrackers, and he almost turned around.

From the bicycle rack on the sidewalk just outside Porter's Store, Coleman could see Mrs. Porter's head through the screen. The rest of her body was covered by the wide sign attached to the middle frame of the door: BY ORDER OF YOUR MAYOR, JUNE 10, 1961. WE'LL HAVE NO TROUBLE WITH THE BLACK FOLKS HERE IN GATOR TOWN. C.P. BRIDGEMAN

Coleman gave a grunt of irritation when he read the sign. There would certainly be no trouble if his grandfather said so. Whatever C.P. said went, just like Coleman's new job. He hadn't asked for it, but before school was out for the summer, his grandfather arranged for him to work at Imogene Porter's store. Truthfully, he enjoyed being away from the cabin and his mother.

Mrs. Porter hired him to work only in the storeroom of the grocery, although the store was attached to the restaurant she also ran. She needed experienced people for the restaurant, she told him, and Coleman didn't qualify.

As he passed the register, Coleman nodded to a skinny woman

with little twin boys hanging onto her legs when they weren't climbing up the counter and a baby plopped on her hip. The skinny woman was trying to pay Mrs. Porter for her groceries, but the two little boys, their mouths drooling chocolate, kept arguing over who was going to get what was left in the hard-candy jar on the counter. "Stop that, Bubba! Buddy, get down now! Y'all don't need no more candy!" the skinny mother hollered at her twins.

Mrs. Porter tried to help by giving the boys her evil eye, but the two laughing little boys were too busy to notice. Each had a hand stuck in the jar, then one began to pinch the other. Mrs. Porter's eyebrows squeezed out an even more sinister look, right up in their candy-coated faces. "Y'all better get out of that jar. You know what too much candy does to you?" She opened her mouth and spat her false teeth onto the counter. "This!"

"Oooh! Yucky!" The twins jerked back and the jar came with them, joining them together like one body with two identical heads.

Mrs. Porter picked up her teeth. "Yes sirree bobtail, one of these days, y'all gonna come in here and have," she pointed a plump finger at her pink gums—"no teeth!"

Then, putting her teeth back in her mouth, she helped the mother get her boys' hands unstuck from the jar. When one of the boys came loose, Mrs. Porter lost her balance and knocked over the suntan-lotion display. "Lord have mercy," she said, resituating the bottles. "You boys act like some greedy men I know."

Coleman watched from the entrance to the storeroom until the unruly family left, and until Mrs. Porter noticed him idle.

"Coleman Puttman Bridgeman III, I know you ain't unloaded them boxes of Blue Plate. I don't see one jar of mayonnaise on that shelf." Her mouth moved in all directions, like she was trying to set her teeth in their proper place.

"I remember the first time you showed me your teeth,"

Coleman said, smiling.

"Lord, child, don't bring up the past." Mrs. Porter started to laugh. "Fell right on top of your handsome granddaddy's pancakes, didn't they?"

"Taught him not to tickle you while you were serving a customer," he said, and both of them laughed, until Mrs. Porter became serious again.

"Um-umh, don't time go by? Had to be five, six years ago, right before your daddy got shot the second time." Mrs. Porter looked steadily at him. There was something soft behind her eyes. He thought she might be getting ready to give him a hug, but he was saved by an annoying greeting coming from the jingle of bells over the door.

"How are you doing, Mrs. Porter?"

"Well hey, Dr. Pauly," Mrs. Porter chirped.

Coleman headed at once for the storeroom.

"I'll see you tonight, Coleman," Dr. Pauly said. It was sort of a question, but intentionally Coleman didn't respond. He couldn't stand it when Dr. Pauly came to the cabin for his every-other-night-sober-up-his-mother therapy.

"He looks a little put out with you, Dr. Pauly," Mrs. Porter observed, but whatever she said after that was silenced by the closing of the storeroom door.

"Put out" wasn't the half of it. If Charles Robert Pauly brought his mother one more damn Whitman's Sampler, he'd personally cram the chocolates down the shrink's throat.

The first thing his mother said to him when he arrived home from work was "I haven't been drinking." Then she spent a good thirty minutes ironing a white cotton dress and went to put it on.

Coming back, she asked him, "How do I look?"

He studied the dress, its little flowers sewn in purple thread around a collar high enough to hide something sacred. "Fine," he said, but he thought she looked beautiful.

His mother seemed satisfied. She stuck her finger into the Creole sauce she had on the stove and tasted it. She seemed satisfied with that, too. "Do you like Charles Robert?" She drew a slow, rhythmic circle into the sauce with a wooden spoon.

He didn't answer.

"He's a good man," she said.

The sauce had a spicy smell, and the aroma of homemade rolls came from the oven. The rolls were his favorite, and the last time she made them was long before his father's death. But now they were for Dr. Pauly, not Coleman.

Through the screen door, he could see the flowers blooming profusely in the yard. He thought of the white rose he and Fig had planted on his father's grave the day after the funeral. The rosebush was quite large by now, but he was sure his mother hadn't seen it. She never visited his father's grave. Her lack of attention to the hallowed place was one more thing he held against her.

"How much do you like Dr. Pauly?" he asked.

"I like him very much."

"Do you love him?"

"I don't know. I think I could love him."

"More than you loved Daddy?"

"I don't know, Coleman. Your daddy was—."

"Crazy. I've heard it before." He looked down the hall to where the door opened into his mother's bedroom, remembering. He wanted to hurt her. "At least my crazy daddy wasn't a drunk."

He expected a different reaction, her usual bleating denial and blame, but she didn't give it. His mother raised her hand to the flowered collar of her dress, staring at nothing for a long moment. "He was like two different people," she said, as if she was trying to explain it to herself. "I never knew which person a day would bring."

"Yes. Good days, bad days," he said, moving away from her. "We still have them, don't we?"

The Creole sauce popped and splattered on the stove top. His mother turned down the burner and began to wipe up the mess. "Your daddy loved you, Coleman."

"He loved you, too, but you killed him." He said it in meanness, to get to her. No one really knew what happened in the bedroom that night, except maybe his mother, unless she'd been too drunk.

She left the kitchen then, for some other room in the cabin, but he thought she'd come back for the last word. In fact, he was counting on it.

When she appeared again, she was holding a vase of white roses. "Fig gave me these for the table tonight. They came from your father's grave."

He was furious at Fig. She wasn't worthy of a single rose from the grave of his father. Offering them to her was almost like forgetting his father altogether. Well, he wouldn't forget, and he wouldn't let his mother forget. If he did, she might run off with the damned shrink, and leave him. Didn't Fig realize that?

Fig would tell Coleman he ought to show some mercy. Fig would say Coleman was condemning Sarah Neal, like she'd condemned the black man his father had saved, and that two wrongs don't make a right. But Fig was the one who was wrong.

His mother's eyes were fixed on the roses. "I loved your father," she said.

Coleman snatched up the wooden spoon and began to stir the

sauce. "Then why did you kill him?" he prodded.

This time, her reaction was her usual one.

"You know who killed him!"

"Tell me again," he said, resuming control of her. He tightened his grip on the spoon and drove it hard around the sides of the pan with a painful pleasure.

"If it hadn't been for the—."

"It was you who pulled the trigger."

"No, I tried to take the gun away." But she didn't appear sure of that at all.

"You shot him."

"Oh, please understand! I don't know if I shot him or not." She seemed to tumble again into a crevice of doubt, and he did not intend to let her climb out of it, not even when she put her head in her hands and began to pray softly, "Hail Mary, full of grace."

"How can you pray?" he asked her in a voice that was condemning enough to shame her.

But this time, he struck the heart of her faith. Salvation. "Because I'm a sinner, Coleman," she said coldly and without apology. "If I wasn't a sinner, I wouldn't need prayer, would I?"

Damn the last word! It was always hers. He pushed out of the screen door and headed for the inlet, certain that as soon as he was out of her sight, his mother would trade in her prayers for the solace of a bottle of whiskey.

He walked along the shoreline, fuming. When he saw Charles Robert's car pull into the driveway, he turned to go back to the cabin, determined to expose his mother to the psychologist as nothing but a drunk. He couldn't wait to cram that reality down the shrink's throat.

He found Charles Robert with his mother, an arm around her slumped shoulders, their backs to him. They stood together, talking quietly near the dining room table ablaze with candles. The smell of roses and burned shrimp Creole drifted through the kitchen, and he saw the Whitman's Sampler on the counter.

His mother turned to face him, her eyes red from tears or maybe whiskey, he didn't know which.

"Oh, Coleman, I'm sorry," she said, so unexpectedly that he was put off balance.

"Coleman, your mother needs you," Charles Robert butted in.

He found his equilibrium again. "All she needs is a whiskey bottle. Can't you see she's drunk right now?"

Charles Robert touched his mother's shoulder. "She's not drunk. She has a problem, yes. But right now she's not drunk." Before he could stop it, Dr. Pauly touched him too, a firm grip on his arm, like he cared.

Coleman jerked away and turned to the counter. In his view was the box of candy. He picked it up and threw it at the doctor, hitting him in the middle of his chest. Pieces of candy scattered to the counter and floor as Dr. Pauly stood there, stunned. Instantly, Coleman regretted it, but he couldn't say so. He wanted to run from the room but he couldn't make his feet move. Instead he shouted at Dr. Pauly: "You sonofabitch!"

"Coleman!" his mother cried. She raised her hand as if she was going to slap him.

Charles Robert grabbed her wrist, took her hand in his, and turned to the boy. "Coleman, can't we start again?"

"Start what?" he said, trying for command of himself, but his lips started to quiver.

The doctor went over to the dining room table and pulled out a chair. "Isn't this your place? Come and eat with us."

Coleman glanced at his mother, her hands at her throat, fingering the flowered collar of her dress. "Coleman, do you know how much I love you?"

The words startled him. He couldn't think of an answer. He tried to resist the shrink leading him to the table, but inside his legs felt like rubber, so he let himself be led. He sat there, through the burned meal, not tasting it, not listening to the sounds of his mother's nervous prattle, not acknowledging Dr. Pauly's presence. Instead, he was remembering that his mother had said she loved him.

Then he came to his senses. Earlier she had said she loved his father, and now she might love Charles Robert. And how many times before had she told him she loved God? He was sure the only thing his mother really loved was the bottle. Couldn't Charles Robert and God see that?

In fact, he suspected that his mother thought of the bottle constantly. She rarely left the cabin unless it came close to empty, becoming steadily more agitated as its contents lowered. Finally, she would make up a reason to drive the Bel Air into town, and then return with a full one. Oh, he had his mother pegged! The bottle was the only thing she hungered for, and the only thing that filled her. There was no room left inside her to love him.

10

After Coleman had gone to his room, Charles Robert stood next to Sarah Neal as she felt around for the final plate in the soapy sink.

"Coleman hates me," she said, handing the sudsy plate to Charles Robert.

He reached over to turn on the faucet, then rinsed off the soap. For more than ten years, he'd solved difficulties in other people he cared little or nothing for, because he felt the mission of it. But this woman had struck him differently from the start. He was pulled, like a magnet, toward her.

"Coleman hates me. He thinks I killed Putt," Sarah Neal was saying. "But it couldn't have been me!"

Charles Robert set down the plate and turned her face toward him. "That's past, Sarah Neal."

"But did I do it, Charles Robert? Did I kill him?"

She let him take her in his arms. "Sh, sh. Let it go," he said, relishing her vulnerability. For a long time, he had been positive he loved this woman. He was positive he could fix her, too, if she would let him.

From the first moment he met her, in the shadow of Putt's misfortune, he'd been attracted to her. He saw that she needed his help as much as Putt had, but he was an ethical clinical psychologist and a Christian who believed in the sanctity of marriage. He often reminded himself that she was Putt's wife, yet beneath the reminder was the truth. He wanted Sarah Neal every time he saw her. Cold showers and prayer still followed his visits to the Bridgeman cabin.

"I want to let it go, but I can't," Sarah Neal said, pressing her face into his chest. "I need a drink, Charles Robert, just one."

"A drink's not the answer."

She pulled away from him and hit her small fist on the counter. "Don't tell me what to do."

"You promised you'd try to quit, Sarah Neal." He thought he sounded like a disappointed adolescent.

"What do you know about how hard I try?"

"Oh, I know you try," he said, wanting to redeem himself. He moved closer. "And I know it's a hard thing to do."

"Yes," she said. "Too hard." She stepped toward the cabinet where she hid her whiskey and took out the bottle.

"You don't need that. You have me," he said. "I love you."

"You love me?" Her voice was filled with sarcasm. "How can you love me? Just ask my own son. I'm a drunk, and maybe a murderer."

"But I do love you, drunk or sober, murderer or not. I love you."

"It's some kind of therapy you're trying out."

"Come here." He walked her into the living room, to the carved mahogany buffet that C.P. had bought for Emma long ago. Above it was a large mirror in an ornate gold frame. He turned her toward it.

"That is Sarah Neal Bridgeman, the woman I love." He took a strand of her hair between his fingers, exposing her temple, and kissed her there. "Sarah Neal Bridgeman is all new, and starting over."

She let go of a long sigh. "I don't look very new, and I don't know if it's possible to start over," she said, "but you ask anybody, Charles Robert. Loving me is the kiss of death."

"Okay," he said, and kissed her again. The woman he'd wanted for so long was finally in his arms. He could take a little risk.

In his room, Coleman lay in the dark thinking about the burned meal and how hungry he was because he'd eaten none of it. He thought about going back into the kitchen to pick up the scattered pieces of candy, but his mother would probably be there, cradling the bottle in her arms as if it was her child. Then he thought of his father and his mother's tiresome claims about the reason her husband was dead. All of it made him anxious. Like his father, the life he should have had was being stolen from him.

He knew what his grandfather would say: "Swallow it like a man." Except it seemed too much to swallow.

Still hungry, he remembered the candy again and went to the kitchen. His mother wasn't there, but nor were the scattered pieces. It was as if someone unknown had sneaked in and taken even those from him.

When he arrived at work the next day, Mrs. Porter was counting yesterday's money. "Mornin', Coleman. How's your mama?"

Earlier, peddling his bicycle to her store, he'd already decided how he would answer her usual grilling.

"Better," he said.

Mrs. Porter appeared disappointed and went back to counting. "Let's see, where was I? One hundred fifty-two, fifty-four, -five, and -six. And how's Charles Robert?"

"How would I know?"

"Are you sassin' me, Coleman Bridgeman?"

"No, ma'am. I don't know how Dr. Pauly is today. I guess he was okay last night." But even the mention of last night unsteadied him.

"Oh?"

"When he came for dinner."

"Sarah Neal cooked?"

"Yes, ma'am."

"What?"

"Shrimp Creole."

"Umm, umm! And what for dessert?"

"The candy you sold him. He gave it to her."

"Must be nice for Sarah Neal to cook for somebody again."

"She already cooks for me."

"Don't play dumb with me, Mr. Bridgeman. You're old enough to know what I'm talkin' about. If the lovebug ain't bit you yet, it soon will, good-lookin' boy like you."

He made a move toward the storeroom, thinking of the girl with the kittens. He'd been almost as rude to her as he'd been to Dr. Pauly. Fig would say that if he kept on like that, he wouldn't have a friend in the world except him. Of course, he didn't have any friends anyway. His unbalanced family had seen to that.

"What should I do, Mrs. Porter?"

"Better ask that of your granddaddy, honey. Forty years ago that man gave a heart attack to every girl at Gator Town High School. He's the one to give you some pointers."

"I mean, what should I do in the storeroom?"

"Umh. Well, it's a good day for you, Coleman. Got a new man to help you unpack the boxes. He's been workin' real hard since I hired him this mornin'."

When Coleman went into the back room, a black man was sitting on one of the boxes. The first thing Coleman noticed was the shirt he wore and its army patch with the insignia of sergeant. The second thing was that the man was smoking a cigarette from a newly slit box.

The black man jumped up when he saw Coleman, and threw the cigarette toward a corner of the room. "Man, I thought you was the boss lady," he said, wiping his forehead in relief. The cigarette made a sizzle sound, and a lick of flame sprung up on a scrap of paper too close to it.

"You burn up this place and you'll be in a heap of trouble," Coleman said. He was a good foot taller than the man, and that gave him a sense of authority.

"I ain't burned it up yet." The man pulled another cigarette from the pocket of the army shirt and lit it. "And I ain't gonna be in no trouble unless you tell."

"Where'd you get that?"

"Over yonder," he said, pointing to a stack of boxes, each marked with I'D WALK A MILE FOR A CAMEL. "She got plenty."

"I mean where'd you get that shirt?" Coleman picked up an angled knife and slit open a box. "You weren't in the war."

The man looked irritated. "I never been out of war, honky child."

"I asked you about the shirt."

The man seemed to poke fun at Coleman's curiosity. He looked up toward the ceiling and grinned. "Got it on the day I was saved."

"Saved?"

"By the Lord Jesus Christ. He's the one sent me here. He's the one struck down them white fools in my path. He's the one—."

"Never mind!" He'd had enough Jesus talk from his mother. This wasn't a man his father would save. "Put these cartons on the shelves up front. You don't get paid for doing nothing," he ordered in a superior tone that would have made his grandfather proud.

"Hold this while I do, honky child." He handed Coleman the cigarette he was smoking and gathered up an armload of Camel cartons for the front of the store.

Coleman took a drag off the cigarette, coughed, and put it out. Then he made a forceful slit with the knife into a container of cereal boxes, thinking it was too bad the new hire wasn't the man his father had saved, because right now he had a weapon in his hand. But just in case, when the man came back to the storeroom, Coleman decided to ask him his name.

"What you got to know for?" the man responded, his suspicious eyes on Coleman.

"A person's got to call somebody something."

"Ain't y'all already got a name for me?"

"Maybe so," Coleman said sarcastically. "But I'll call you Sarge anyway."

"Yeah? You and who else?" the man asked, as if he dared an argument.

Coleman decided to ignore the remark. This was just a lazy colored man of no account, not worth getting upset over, and he didn't need another war of words. He already had one going on with his mother.

He scooped up an armload of boxes and took them up front, anxious to get his work done. He was thinking of the girl again and how he might see her and make amends.

Mrs. Porter was behind the counter, bagging groceries for a woman customer and watching him from the corner of her eye as he quickly unloaded the cereal onto the shelves.

"Lord Coleman," she said, after the customer had left. "The way you're chompin' to get finished, you must have somebody special to see. Wouldn't be that little Saylor girl, Anna, would it?"

"Anna?"

"You haven't seen her yet? She and her daddy—that's Eloise's brother—are opening up the place for the summer. It's the first time anybody's been there since your daddy's funeral."

"I saw her."

Mrs. Porter grinned. "Pretty little thing. Her mama recently died, so I hear. They say her mama was the only decent Saylor ever lived, except for the girl. I hear she's sweet, too. What do you think?"

"I don't care if she's sweet or not, Mrs. Porter. I'll bring out some more Cheer. It looks to be a little low." He started off.

"Whoa, boy," she said, nodding toward the storeroom. "Is he doin' his job back there?"

"I guess so."

"Long as he don't take nothin.' You watch him now."

"What'd you hire him for if you thought he was going to steal from you?"

"Don't you sass me one more time, Mr. Bridgeman. The good Lord says 'Feed the hungry,' and that's what he said he was, hungry."

"So you fed him."

"I fed him, and he's workin' it out."

"You don't even know him. I'll bet he never told you his name."

"The good Lord did not say you got to know somebody's name to feed him. Anyway, he ain't dangerous. I'd bet my store on that," she said, just as Sarge came through the swinging doors carrying a couple of boxes.

"Miz Boss lady," he purred. "What you want me to do with these?"

"Second shelf, over there," she said. "By the way, what's your name?"

"Peoples call me Sarge, Miz Boss lady," he said, giving Coleman a smirk.

"Sarge? Were you in the war?"

"Yes, ma'am, a cook. Lookin' after them hungry white boys was my specialty."

She glanced toward Coleman. "Well, I declare," she said, clearly impressed.

After work, Coleman went directly to the fish house, where Fig stood in front of the window, watering a flat of seedlings set on the sill. "I might have found the man my daddy saved." Coleman said.

A pale orange ray of light from the sunset lay across Fig's hands as he set down the water pitcher. "Is that so?"

"Well?" Coleman waited for Fig's reaction. "What do you think of that?"

Fig took the shears off their hook on the wall and began to polish the blades with a rag. "What do I think of what?"

"You know what I mean, Fig," Coleman persisted. "Mrs. Porter just hired a black man. He's wearing an army jacket and he was talking about being saved."

"What makes him the one?"

Coleman shrugged. He didn't really know what made Sarge the one, except for the shirt and that he told Mrs. Porter he'd been in the army. It was mostly a feeling he had, that Sarge was a person who'd let somebody sacrifice his life for his. He told Fig that, but Fig said it wasn't enough evidence.

"There are lots of people who'll let somebody die for them," Fig said.

Annoyed by his lack of interest, Coleman started rummaging under the rollaway bed.

"What in the world you doin'?" Fig asked.

"Looking for the name of the man my daddy saved. It might be in the old newspaper."

"Honey boy, when you gonna let loose of that stuff? That man ain't nowhere but in your head, where Miz Sarah Neal put him. Anyway, Boss burned up that newpaper long time ago."

"But didn't anybody ever say what his name was or where he came from? I need to find him, Fig!"

"Why? You turned into Surelocked Homes? What's any of that gonna change after all this time?"

"I need to see the truth."

Fig hung up the shears and limped toward Coleman. "Be careful, honey boy. It's two ways to see the truth." He pointed to the crucifix hanging over the bookcase. "And Jesus done showed you it ain't but one way that works."

"I know what works," Coleman said. "I don't need a man suffering on a cross to show me."

Fig gave him a cold glare. "Well, maybe you're the monkey that can't see hisself."

"The monkey?"

"There's two kind of monkeys lookin' in a mirror. One of them so high and mighty, he don't see a monkey lookin' back."

"What does he see, then?"

"Whatever he decides to see, but that don't make it true."

"And the second monkey?"

"He's the smart one. What the second monkey sees in the mirror is the same monkey face that's doin' the lookin'."

He didn't know how to respond to Fig. Maybe it didn't matter who his father saved. Maybe he could even forget about it, if his mother would let him. Then he remembered how often he had brought up that awful night to force her into admitting she shot his father. But had she really killed him? Or like the first monkey, was that just the way he'd decided to see it?

Sometimes, he felt things were changing. With his job at the store, he was doing something new, on his own. Yet things weren't changing either. It was as if he had an old enemy on his back who kept dredging up painful things and packing them inside his head to confuse him. If he'd been younger, he might have cried, or he might even have tried a Hail Mary. Now, he was too old for crying, and saying the Hail Mary would be like asking his mother to help him, and he had too much pride for that. If he was too old to cry and too proud to pray, though, there was still one thing he wasn't. He wasn't dumb enough to look in any monkey mirror! He told Fig that.

As usual, he could never get one up on Fig, not even with an insolent remark. Fig patted his shoulder. "Got to look in that mirror one day, honey boy, and see what you don't want to see. But don't worry none. Love will help you bear it."

On his way out, Coleman slammed the fish house door behind him. Halfway up the yard, he turned around and yelled back to Fig: "You're the one who needs to look in the mirror. Love only makes things hurt."

11

From across the inlet, Anna Saylor heard those words. She watched the son of her summer neighbor ascend the manicured yard to a home that held for him, she was sure, as much contention as her own. She saw it in the tight set of his mouth. She heard it hiding beneath the few words he'd said to her. She knew his hidden grief. It was the same as hers. She could tell him her secret, the way she had learned to battle the sting with silent words too private to speak aloud. She could tell him that love not only helped, but also changed things. She didn't think the boy was a true believer, not yet, but she thought she could make him one.

She turned her eyes upward, kneeling on the edge of the Saylor dock. She knelt because she'd seen her mother kneel. She prayed, because she'd seen her mother pray, a mother she still loved. For a while she received no answer, and then all at once, it came. The boy, Coleman Puttman Bridgeman III, needed her help. And she needed his.

He wasn't like those buttoned-down-collared boys from the private school she attended. They were privileged boys, and she was privileged too, enough to have whatever she wanted, her father often told her on his way to the office or a necessary business trip. But "whatever she wanted" wasn't true. She couldn't have her mother back. Not even her rich, political, and very absent father could raise the dead.

She thought her father missed her mother, but twice, after she died, he'd brought a woman home for dinner to fill her empty place. Anna hated each woman for sitting at her mother's table, for dropping crumbs on her mother's lace tablecloth. She wouldn't have spoken to either of them at all if it hadn't been for Ruby whispering in her ear, "Your mama didn't raise no Charlie McCarthy, girl. Talk to the people!" She spoke then, a few polite words, and a relieved goodnight. But when her father said goodnight too, she was left alone, waiting for a loving touch, a hand to hold.

She saw the boy, Coleman, the first night they arrived at the inlet. He was fishing with his grandfather. She watched him turn in her direction and felt the fluff of hope that maybe he'd be a friend. But her father saw them, too. "Stay away from those idiots," he warned her. She didn't ask why. He wouldn't have taken the time to tell her.

The next day, she noticed Fig pruning the roses and recognized him as an honest believer. She asked the boy's name and heard Fig tell her that Coleman needed a friend, too. She'd waited behind the red tips for the boy to appear. Although she startled him and he slapped her open hand, she didn't feel it. She was an optimist. Hope kept his slap from stinging.

That night, Coleman dreamed about Anna Saylor. She was standing on the dock, offering him some sort of dim light in her hands, but when he took it from her, it burst into flames and he had to let it go. He was awakened from the dream by what sounded like the opening of the kitchen door. He thought he saw a light spread from the kitchen into the hall, as if someone was taking food from the refrigerator, but it was probably his mother, drinking again.

Early on Sunday morning, his mother shook him awake.

"Coleman, come out to the porch!" He tried to turn over and go back to sleep, but she wouldn't let him. He followed her outside.

Someone was loading a station wagon in the driveway of the Saylors' cabin. He was disappointed when he thought it might be Anna leaving, but as the car backed out, he could see it wasn't her.

"It's Eloise Saylor, isn't it?" his mother asked, straining to see across the patch of briars to the neighboring cabin.

"It's not her, Mama." Actually, he didn't know who it could be. His grandfather had been sure the only people staying in the cabin were the girl and her father.

"Somebody's staying there. Who is it?"

"Just some girl and her father," he said. "If you'd quit draining the whiskey bottle, you'd remember that Granddaddy told you who it was."

He went inside, and she followed. In the living room, she called to him as he went down the hall to get away from her. "I'm going to quit, Coleman, by next Saturday, when Charles Robert comes for dinner. You'll see. I'm going to fix your favorite rolls again, and the three of us will have a wonderful time."

He could think of nothing worse. He slammed the door to his room and stood for a while, his hands to his ears, until she was silent.

Sarge was half-asleep in the patch of briars between the two cabins, underneath some trumpet vines, thinking about his new name. He rarely slept soundly. In fact, he hadn't had a good night's sleep since he slept on a U.S. Army cot, the first bed he'd lay on that wasn't flat on the floor. Then the woman's voice startled him. He thought she'd discovered the food he stole from her refrigerator and had called the police, but it was a false alarm. She was just up there arguing with somebody.

He rolled to his side to sleep some more, shoving away the opened cans and empty carton of milk, but he was bothered by something in his pants pocket. He stuck in a hand and pulled out Jesus's mama. He'd forgotten she was in there. There was no need to bargain with Jesus anymore. He had found his place, and meant to take advantage of it. He tossed the statue on the sand and started his walk to town.

Monday morning, on his way to work, a short distance from the line of red tips, Coleman imagined Anna in front of him again. This time he would smile at her, or maybe even laugh and touch her shoulder. This time, if she was there, he would do things right. The thought of redeeming himself caused him to pedal faster to the line of trees but Anna wasn't there. He rode a wide circle in front of the red tips, and then another, but the only thing he met was an abrupt rush of wind that blew dust into his face.

At Mrs. Porter's Store, Sarge was leaning against the wall of the storeroom, smoking again. "Why don't you just do the job you're hired to do?" Coleman asked him.

"Already done my part before you got here."

"And what was that? Those boxes over there haven't been touched."

"She ain't told me to do that. She told me to sweep under the front counter, and I done it." Sarge puffed twice on his cigarette. "In a minute, I'm fixin' to go up there and ask her what else she wants."

"She wants you to unload those boxes. So get to it."

"You go spittin' in my face again, honky child, you gonna be sorry." His fingers touched an angled knife stuck in his belt.

"You think that knife makes you a big man? It takes a lot more than that."

"Yeah? What does it take, honky child? Tell me. Do it take being white?"

Coleman could have shrugged it off. He'd almost made up his mind not to bother with Sarge anymore, but he couldn't let the remark stand. "It's courage that makes a hero. Not that you'd understand," he said, turning his back on the man.

Sarge grabbed his shoulder. "No, it don't. Not if you ain't white. Not even in the U.S. Army."

"You weren't in the army. You probably stole that shirt. There's no name on it."

"Maybe I stole it from a white man, huh?"

"Yeah. You weren't in the army."

"How you know so much about who's in the army and who ain't?"

"My daddy was in the war. He had courage. He was a hero."

"Because he was white."

"No! Because he saved a man. He got his brains shot out for somebody like you, and all he got was a damn medal!"

Sarge set a bullet-eyed gaze on the boy. "I never got no medal."

"Because you weren't a hero. And you're lying about being in the war."

Sarge whisked out the knife. "You don't know nothing, honky child. You don't know if I was a hero or not. You ain't seen my scars."

Coleman grabbed his wrist and Sarge dropped the knife. "You don't have any scars," Coleman said, picking it up. "You've never saved anybody."

Sarge glared at him. Then he snatched a can of baked beans from an opened box and stuck it into his jacket pocket, and then another can.

"Put those back! Mrs. Porter hired you because she thought you needed a job, not a free ride."

"Ain't on a free ride, honky child. Only white folks get free rides, and medals, too."

"You lying coward," Coleman said. He pushed the lightweight man to the floor and straddled him, the knife to Sarge's throat.

"Whoa now. I ain't your enemy," Sarge gasped. "I can see you need to kill somebody, honky child, but I ain't the one."

Kill somebody? He was stunned enough to let Sarge go. "Get out! I"ll tell Mrs. Porter you quit."

"Don't want to quit. She still owe me my wage, and I ain't gonna get it if I quit."

"You stole a hell of a lot more than she owes you," Coleman said, moving toward him until they were face to face.

Then Sarge squinted and said, "You sure do favor somebody I used to know. Could be I knew your hero daddy."

Coleman pushed Sarge against the wall, then ran out of the store, with Mrs. Porter hollering after him: "Where do you think you're goin', Mr. Bridgeman? It ain't quittin' time!"

He ran all the way to Fig's place in the garage above C.P.'s house in town. He was positive now, he told Fig. Sarge was the man his father saved. But Fig only gave his shoulder a pat. "Go on back to work, honey boy. It'll help you get all them silly ideas out of your head."

Fig watched Coleman sulk back down the street toward Porter's. He ached for that boy. Only Jesus knew why he loved him so much. Some black folks said it wasn't natural, him loving a white boy like he did. Some black folks said the grandson of a mayor would turn on him one day, but Fig didn't believe them. "A person don't turn on them that raised them" is what he'd said back to them. That, and to put up their wagging tongues until they had something decent to say.

But some black folks said the times were changing, like the song kept singing over the radio. We shall overcome, they said, and when it happened, Fig wouldn't want to be living like he was. He'd ask them what they meant by that. "You working for the boss, ain't you?" And he'd say yes. "You're following his rules, ain't you?" And he'd say yes. "See?" they'd say, "You're oppressed because you ain't white." And he'd say being oppressed didn't have nothin' to do with color. They'd shake their heads and tell him that when the overcoming came, just get out of their way.

That's exactly what he planned to do, because he hadn't told a soul, except Mama Nem found out, long ago, that he was color-blind. She asked him one day, pointing in her books, "What color is this?"

"Red," he answered.

"No, Fig," she said, "it's green." Then she put her palm on the top of his head and laughed in that little glass-bell way she had. "I do believe you're color-blind, sugar."

He started back into the house and noticed the Jeep needed polishing again. The boss didn't like dust, especially the limerock dust that forever lay in wait on the road from Gator Town to the inlet. If the old man was here, he'd wipe a finger through the ashy, silky stuff, and say: "Can't keep nothin' lookin' like its supposed to." Then he would ask Fig, "Didn't he have a job to do?"

But, the boss wasn't here. He was down at the doctor's, where Fig had driven him an hour earlier. "You keep my business to yourself," C.P. had said, huffing up the back steps to the clinic so he wouldn't be seen and thought to be afflicted.

The boss hadn't wanted to go. Fig made the appointment for

him after one too many nights of sweats and vomiting and pain in his chest when he woke Fig to sit with him, when he gripped the sheets and sometimes Fig's hand until the pain subsided. It was then that he wanted Fig to retell the stories about Mama Nem's virtues. Just today, the old man wanted to hear again how his wife had forgiven his unfaithfulness.

"You sure she said that?" C.P. asked in a halted breath that yanked at the center of Fig's own chest.

"She surely said it. Because Jesus told her to."

"Dammit," C.P. gasped, squeezing harder on Fig's fingers. "Jesus ain't behind everythin'!"

"No sir. Just the good stuff."

Waiting now until it was time to pick up his boss, Fig rubbed an olive-colored circle into the dust on the hood of the Jeep and saw his reflection.

"Is you good stuff?" he asked the image.

And the image clearly answered him: "Well sure, Fig. Ain't I always behind you?"

As soon as he got home from work, Coleman's mother called him to the porch. "That girl's on the beach. She's a Saylor. Stay away from her."

When he looked and saw Anna, he headed straight for her, leaving Sarah Neal clutching the sides of her silk kimono.

"The Saylors are enemies, Coleman!" she called after him.

He followed the girl for a while, covering her footprints with his. When he was just behind her, she turned around, and he wasn't sure what to do next.

He looked down at the sand. "I'm sorry about the other day."

"You weren't very nice, but I shouldn't have jumped in front of you like that," she said, reprieving him with a smile. He noticed an open cut just below her knee.

"What happened?"

She seemed surprised. "Oh, I must have scratched myself in the patch of briars. I was cleaning up some old cans and garbage that were left there. Probably by a tramp."

He barely heard what she was saying, with her hair glowing in the sunlight like it was.

"Do you have a handkerchief?"

Of course he didn't. "You could wash it off in the water."

He followed her in, ankle-deep. He had thought she was pretty. Now he saw that she was beautiful. But was she his enemy, like his mother said? And did she know who he was?

"Do you know who I am?" he asked her.

She laughed. "Why? Are you famous?"

He was certain he blushed. "I mean, do you know my name?"

"Yes," she said, giggling, then splashing water on her wound. "Coleman Puttman Bridgeman III."

At first his name didn't seem to faze her, then she looked at him and said, "I heard your father was accidentally killed."

He prepared himself for what she might say next, that she'd also heard his father was crazy.

"My mother was killed, too, in an automobile accident." She was looking at him for some reaction. Again, he didn't know what to say, so she turned for the shore.

"I'm sorry about your mother," he said, rushing to catch up.

Her face brightened. "And I'm sorry about your father. Fig said you loved him a lot."

That surprised him. "How do you know Fig?"

"I saw him working in your yard. He likes cats. He said you liked them, too."

He didn't remember discussing cats with Fig, but he nodded.

"That's why I thought you might want to see the kittens."

"I'd like to see them," he said. "The other day, I was—." He couldn't think how to finish, but she reached for his hand and smiled, as if she knew he'd follow her anywhere.

They had to stoop into a small doorway in the foundation of the Saylors' house. The kittens stared wide-eyed next to a big orange cat. Anna took up one and put it to her cheek. It set its tiny claws into her neck, but she didn't seem to mind. When she tried to pull it away, it tightened its hold on her, and it took some effort to loosen the mewling thing, but when she offered it to him, he couldn't take it. Something about it reminded him of his mother, and he knew he had to get out of there.

12

Charles Robert surprised Sarah Neal by coming over when she hadn't expected him. He walked through the unlocked door to the kitchen while she was pouring herself another whiskey. How had she missed the sound of his car? Now Charles Robert was glaring at her, talking to her in such an angry way.

"Listen to me, Sarah Neal. Coleman is suffering because of your drinking. You can't be a mother to him if you're always drunk."

"So I'm a bad mother, too?" she snapped back. "You seem to be forgetting that none of this is my fault." It was a line he'd once agreed with. Maybe it would still work.

"Quit blaming everybody else for your mistakes."

"I haven't made any mistakes!"

He gave her a cold, hard stare. "I can't deal with this anymore, Sarah Neal." He punched the refrigerator door with his fist. It was so unlike him. "I'm sick of hearing about it, and I'm sick of seeing you drunk."

She replied with sarcasm: "You said you loved me drunk or sober."

"I do. I always will." He moved toward her, softening a little, until she took a swallow of her drink. At that, his previous mood returned. "But I have to let you go, Sarah Neal."

She didn't want him to let her go, but she had too much pride to admit it. "Then don't come over here again." She expected him to do what he always did when he realized he'd upset her: apologize, and take her into his arms.

"Until you make a choice, until you choose the love of your son and my love, too, over that damn bottle, I won't be coming over here again."

"Then go on and leave."

She was amazed when he did.

Sarah Neal hated the part of Gator Town where the liquor store was, and she hated buying it herself, but what could she do? Even though Charles Robert was opposed to her drinking, she'd been able to manipulate him into buying her whiskey by reminding him of her suffering, or withholding visits from the man she knew adored her. She'd felt some guilt. It was not the right way to do things, but sometimes it was the only way she could have the bottled numbness she craved, a ravenous numbness that began snaking over her, little by little, beginning the first time she saw the damage that being a hero could cause.

The man who ran the liquor store stood behind the counter, eyeing her with a curling grin, as he did the last time she came in. The same unsavory men hung around the door, red-eyed, thick-tongued, calling her honey and sugar. Didn't they know who she was, that she was high class compared to them?

Then she realized she ought to be glad they didn't know her. If C.P. ever got wind of her being down here, he'd be furious. Not because he'd be worried about her, but only that he'd be concerned about his family's reputation. Ha! Couldn't C.P. see what a farce that was? He had a crazy son who'd stripped naked in front of the town, and might even have been guilty of rape—despite that Eloise made herself available to any male on two legs.

At times Sarah Neal tried to forgive and forget all of that, but she never seemed able to. Forgetting, and especially forgiving, would erase the justification for her drinking. Without the excuses, she'd have to look at herself differently. It was easier to blame somebody else, especially somebody she'd never set eyes on. Whoever the damn black man was, she was positive he'd never said thank you to Putt or even I'm sorry. Oh, how her hero had suffered for such an ingrate!

Setting her bottle on the counter to pay for it, she thought that tonight was the first time she'd considered Putt's suffering more than her own.

She was just out of the door, hurrying down the dark sidewalk, when someone grabbed her and tried to take her brown bag of whiskey. He was a younger man with boyish hands that raked across her chest for the bottle, ripping her blouse and exposing the crucifix that hung from her neck. When the man saw it, he backed off. "Jesus!" he cried, "forgive me," and immediately ran into the shadows.

Clutching the treasured bag, she hustled to her car, locked the doors, and sat there a minute to catch her breath. She tucked in her torn blouse as best she could, covering the cross and the medal behind it, then looked into the rearview mirror to check her face. It looked worn, frightened, and old. She wanted to be new again. She wanted to start over, like Charles Robert said.

Down the dingy street, above a few flat-top buildings, she could see the tiny cross of St. Michael's and thought of the rose window inside, depicting the archangel kneeling before the Virgin Mary with sword in hand to destroy the enemy that no one could see. Her own enemy was here, right in her own hand, the brown bag with its deceiving offer of immediate comfort. She laid her forehead against the steering wheel and cried.

When he arrived at work, Coleman passed the interior doorway that joined Imogene Porter's store to her restaurant and heard his grandfather's voice. "Umm! Imogene, these pancakes is even good when it ain't Saturday." He winked at the chief, who sat across the table, and the chief gave a grunt of a laugh.

C.P. stuffed a forkful of pancakes dripping with maple syrup into his mouth. "You been a widow too long," he said, the shadow of Mrs. Porter's large frame on his face. "Somebody ought to be wakin' up to your pancakes every day of the week." He reached to tickle her thigh.

"Could be you, C.P., you had any sense." She giggled like a girl as she shoved his hand away. "I can't take credit for these, though. My new cook made them. You know he was a mess sergeant during the war?"

"That so?" C.P. wadded up a paper napkin stuck to the syrup on his fingers and wiped his mouth. "And how's Coleman doin' for you?" he asked, poking his sticky fingers into the glass of ice water to clean them.

"He's doin' fine, but you need to lighten up on the boy. Coleman's got a good heart."

C.P. dried his fingers on his pants leg. "A good heart don't do squat without a winnin' hand to go with it."

"It ain't everybody thinks that way," Imogene said, looking directly at him. "Some people bet their whole life on a good heart, even if it don't get noticed. Anyway, I think Coleman has himself a little girlfriend."

Just inside the store, loading the shelves, Coleman cringed.

Why couldn't Mrs. Porter keep her mouth shut!

"Saylor girl?" C.P. stretched back from the table, interested. Chief Harper went into a fit of coughing.

"Think so," Imogene said. She slapped the chief on the back, picked up the syrup bottle he'd knocked over, and hollered toward the kitchen. "Sarge, come on out here and wipe up after the chief."

"The Saylor girl," C.P. repeated, not noticing the syrup rolling toward his empty plate. "I was afraid of that."

"Is Eloise back?" Chief Harper asked, as if he was afraid too.

"Oh, for heaven's sake!" Imogene grabbed the wet rag Sarge had come with and began to mop up the syrup. "How'd you get to be chief anyway? You don't know a thing that goes on around here." She bumped into Sarge, standing hunched-shouldered behind her. "By the way, this here's my new cook. Name's Sarge."

The two men barely nodded to him, but Sarge, with his eyes glued to the Gator Town police patch on the chief's uniform, lit up like they were all old friends just reunited. "How y'all been doin' lately?"

The men glared at Sarge as if he was a polecat about to crawl under their table.

Imogene slapped the wet rag against Sarge's apron. "Take this on back to the kitchen."

"Yes ma'am," Sarge said. He left, grinning.

The chief scratched his nose and focused on Imogene. "So Eloise isn't here?"

"She ain't here—yet," Imogene said, irritated. "But she's comin'. And the girl's her niece. Anythin' else the chief of police needs to know?" She bent close to C.P.'s ear. "It'll be hell for Sarah Neal and poor little old Coleman, too, when that woman gets here." She bustled through the adjoining entrance to the store without noticing Coleman.

He watched the big woman fiddle with the cash register while she glanced into the restaurant, her eyes resting lovingly on his grandfather. She had a heart the size of Texas, but it hadn't made her smart.

Coleman was galled that Sarge was still around. Mrs. Porter had obviously shifted him over to work the diner, a ridiculous move. He had to warn her. A person like Sarge could take advantage of anybody with a heart as big as hers and destroy everything she had.

He went over to her and said, "That Sarge is going to steal you blind."

She looked up at him and cocked her head. "No, he ain't. That's prejudiced, Coleman Bridgeman. One thing nobody can say about me is I'm prejudiced."

No, he thought, maybe *stupid* would be a better word, but he didn't say that. Instead, he started for the storeroom.

"Coleman," she called after him. "I'll tell you what. You go ahead and take off early tomorrow. The county fair's in town and I got two free tickets if you want to take somebody." She must have been feeling sorry for him, because she turned all mushy and came over to squeeze his shoulder. "It don't seem like it now, honey," she said, "but bide your time. After all the trials and errors, it's a justice comin' in the end."

A justice coming? He didn't believe it. But maybe tomorrow he would take her up on the tickets to the fair. And maybe he would invite Anna.

The next morning, at barely dawn, Coleman dressed in the dark and went out onto the porch to look across the inlet. He wasn't surprised to see the soft-edged shape of Anna sitting on the Saylors' dock. Fog rose from the flat water and for a moment separated her from his gaze. But even in the floating fog, he imagined her watching him, and the idea of that connection set loose a rush of heat and a throbbing heart that he understood as a yearning for attachment. He closed his eyes to picture what love with Anna would be like, and opened them a few seconds later on the whistling call of a bobwhite. And there she was, in the middle of the long yard, between the soft pastel of Fig's flowers and the sun rising red behind her.

When he stepped off the porch, she began to walk toward him, smiling. When they reached each other, he noticed the neatly defined corners of her mouth pinched into tiny dimples. He wanted to kiss her but he didn't know how. "Did you walk across the water?" he asked, almost believing she could.

"I came through the patch, but no blood this time. See?" She pointed below the hems of her cotton shorts to her slender legs. Perfectly shaped legs, he thought. All of her perfectly shaped.

"I cleaned up the circle again. I don't know where the trash comes from, but isn't it beautiful now, in the early light?"

He looked toward the circle of sand. The thorned scrub was overgrown with deep violet flowers and the sand was white as milk. "Yes. Beautiful."

"Come with me."

He followed her up the yard, past the big live oak, and down the dirt road to the thick border of red tips. They bent underneath the trees into a space where nothing grew and dead leaves from past autumns covered the ground. She sat down. He sat beside her.

She took his hand, her fingers laced in his, and he felt a warmth in the clasp of their hands so intense that for several moments it prevented him from breathing.

"I want this to be our place, Coleman," she whispered, as if they were in a church. "Whenever we need to, we'll come here, and we'll say anything that ought to be said, anything at all."

"I don't have anything to say," he whispered back, but it wasn't true. He didn't know how to tell her that she was all he thought about.

"Well, I have something to say." Anna looked at him intently. "I know your father was wounded in the war."

He was suddenly angry but he couldn't show it or she might take her hand from his. He asked softly, "Who told you that?"

"Aunt Eloise."

"Is she here?"

"Yes, to stay with me for a few days, while Daddy's away on business."

"What else did she tell you?"

"Just that your daddy was . . . not quite right. And that I should stay away from you."

Eloise, the enemy, had sneaked in again. In a voice that was no longer a whisper, he said, "Your aunt's a liar." His statement seemed to stun her. Still, she kept hold of his hand until he pulled it away and stood. "I've got to go."

"Wait. I don't want to stay away from you. Your daddy couldn't help it if he was shot in the head."

"I've got to go!"

"Why are you always running away from me?"

Her words trailed him as he pushed through the boughs of red tips. He felt vulnerable, almost naked. She'd unwrapped a piece of him, and he had allowed it. He did not intend to let her unwrap more.

Imogene was closing up the store side of Porter's when the bell over the door jingled. An attractive red-haired woman in large sunglasses emerged from a red Thunderbird convertible and came in.

The woman stopped to pick up some suntan lotion and a *True Story* magazine, but Imogene was busy counting money and didn't look up when she said, "Y'all come on in."

The woman took off her sunglasses. "How're you, Imogene?"

"Eloise Saylor! Where in the world did you get that red hair?"

"From a bottle, honey. Bottles cover up lots of things, you know." She tucked in the corners of her mouth. "So how's little Miss Sarah Neal doing?"

"You're sassy as you ever was, Eloise."

"I hear C.P.'s still runnin' Gator Town. That obnoxious Fig still work for him?"

"He'll be with C.P. till he dies, I reckon. I hear you're takin' care of your niece for a while."

"Gator Town's never kept any secrets from you, has it?" Eloise laughed. "Well, maybe one."

"What do you mean?" Imogene asked, insulted by the prospect.

Eloise noticed Sarge, dressed in a cook's apron, listening in the doorway to the restaurant. "Who's that?"

Imogene gave Sarge a wave of her hand that meant "get back to work." "That's my new cook," she said.

"I could use a cook. I don't know a thing about makin' a meal, and I'm sure little old Anna's gonna need somethin' to nourish her. Do you have anythin' frozen, Imogene?"

Sarge edged in carefully. "Uh, pardon me, Miz Imogene. You want me to slap the beef tonight with my best chef barbecue sauce, the one with old Jack Daniels stirred right inside?"

"Jack Daniels?" Eloise asked, interested.

"Yes ma'am." Sarge grinned. "If Miz Imogene don't mind, I'd be proud for you to taste some of it. Got some right back there in the kitchen. Good old Jack Daniels, uh-huh!"

Eloise gave a mocking smile. "Never mind the frozen stuff, Imogene. Maybe I'll just borrow your chef for a while."

"Be fine with me," Sarge said, excited. "I mean, on my off-time from Porter's, of course. Fact is, I been thinkin' about hirin' myself out to cook for some sweet, pretty white lady like you. Maybe even drive for you, too. I know how to drive red convertibles." He pointed at the front window. "Just like the one you came in."

"Go on back to the kitchen, Sarge," Imogene snapped. "Miz Saylor's just talking."

Sarge moved away, but when Eloise left, Imogene noticed him at the window, watching as she drove off in her shiny red car.

Later in the day, Mrs. Porter gave Coleman the fair tickets and told him to take off early. He shoved them into his pocket as he passed the drugstore next to Porter's, where most of the teenagers hung out. He desperately wanted to take Anna to the fair if he hadn't ruined it by running away from her.

Outside the drugstore window, he noticed the rack of greeting cards and went in to finger through them. He'd found one he liked when a voice came from behind, "Who's that for, Bridgeman?" a tall boy taunted.

"Mind your own business, Freddie."

"You taking anybody to the fair, Coleman?" asked a smaller boy who was standing next to Freddie.

"Maybe."

"Maybe who?" Freddie asked, raising his eyebrows.

"Nobody you know."

"Yeah? Well, I know who you ain't takin'. Anna Saylor, because I'm taking her. My mama's fixed it up with her aunt."

"You wasn't going to take her anyway, was you, Coleman?" the smaller boy said in Coleman's defense.

"Hell no!" He got out of the drugstore as fast as he could.

Anna rubbed on a little suntan oil and said to her aunt, beside her on the dock, "You wouldn't lie to me, would you?"

Eloise looked up from her *True Story* magazine. "Lie about what?"

"Coleman Bridgeman said you lied when you told me about his father. What did he mean?"

"I have no earthly idea," Eloise said, flipping through the pages. "It was your daddy who told me to keep you away from that boy."

"But why?"

"Because crazy runs in families, that's why." She took a swallow of her beer. "Besides, his mama's a drunk."

"Coleman isn't crazy."

"Your daddy said he was crazy enough to punch out the son of the city council chairman, that Freddie Feezer, over something Freddie said about Coleman's background. Of course, big boss, Mr. C.P. Bridgeman smoothed it over." She noticed Anna eyeing her curiously. "That's all according to your daddy, of course. I personally have no idea what goes on around here, and I don't care either."

"Hey there, miz pretty white lady." The voice came from down the dock.

"Who's that?" Anna asked.

"I guess he was serious about cooking for me," Eloise said as Sarge come toward them, a sack in his hand.

"Here's your barbecue sauce, pretty lady, and Miz Imogene

said I can cook dinner for y'all if you want me to."

An hour later, Eloise and Anna sat at the table in the dining room of the Saylors' house. Sarge stood watching as they picked at what he'd prepared.

"What's this called, this stuff next to the barbecue?" Eloise asked.

"Scrambled eggs and pig brains. Ain't it good? My auntie taught it to me."

"Ugh!" Anna spat a mouthful back onto her plate.

"I agree," Eloise whispered, and then remembered. "Oh, I meant to tell you, Anna. You have a date for the fair with Freddie Feezer. I've already fixed it up with his mama."

"But I don't know Freddie Feezer, Aunt Eloise."

"Well, that's too bad. He'll be here soon, so change your clothes."

Eloise and Sarge stood in the yard as Anna drove off with Freddie. "I guess I'd better pay you for your trouble," Eloise said, and offered him a fifty-cent piece.

Sarge looked stunned. "You supposed to be a rich, sweet white lady," he said.

"And you were supposed to be a cook," Eloise retorted, and walked back to the house with her nose in the air.

Coleman hadn't wanted to go to the fair without taking Anna, but Fig said he'd go with him. Reluctantly, Coleman agreed, thinking maybe he would catch a glimpse of the girl.

Colorful lights and music were in the air as he and Fig walked from a parking lot filled with cars toward the fairgrounds. Fig had to use the back entrance, marked COLORED, but they made plans to meet up again at the Shoot the Ducks booth. Coleman had already won a stuffed monkey by the time he caught sight of Anna getting off the Ferris wheel.

She must have seen him, too. She was tugging Freddie along in Coleman's direction.

"Reckon no girl wanted to come with the son of a crazy man, huh, Bridgeman?" Freddie sneered when they were close. Coleman made a fist and took a step toward the boy, but Fig pulled him back.

"That's not true, Freddy," Anna said. "I'd have come with him if he'd asked me."

"Well, he didn't, so let's go." Freddie yanked her arm.

She walked away with him, but she turned to look back at Coleman and smiled. The whole night was worth that one smile.

13

At C.P.'s house in town, Fig went to his room over the garage and sat the stuffed monkey Coleman had given him on his bed. Its black button eyes aimed toward him. He picked up the hand mirror from his bureau and held it in front of the monkey's face. "What do you see, old fellow?"

"Looks like a monkey, Fig," he said, talking for the toy. He chuckled at himself and went down to check on C.P.

The boss lay in bed, sleeping and sweating profusely. Fig stood beside him for a few minutes until C.P. awoke.

"How was the damn fair?" the Boss asked. Fig could see he was in pain.

"Fine. I got me a monkey. How you feelin'?"

C.P. sat bent over on the edge of the bed, massaging his chest, a grimace on his face.

"We're goin'," Fig said. "Come on, Boss. Can't wait no longer."

"Ain't goin' nowhere. Tell me again what you heard my Emma say before she died."

Fig gave an exasperated breath. "Heard her say she always loved you and forgave you for everythin'. And right now I hear her again. She sayin', 'Fig, get that darned old fool down to the hospital. Now!'"

C.P. sat straight up then. "Hell's bells, I'm fine. Fact is I feel so good I'm gonna take the boy fishin' tomorrow. Can't let you and that stuffed monkey outdo me."

Later in the night, even in the dead of sleep, C.P. heard the sirens whine. At first he thought they were part of his dream, a dream in which he was having Chief Harper drag the river for the body of some Gator Town redneck who'd been knocked over the side of his own damn boat by a stranger he'd taken fishing. In the dream, the sirens fit the redneck's screams as he wrestled with a strange kind of black-fingered thing that kept coming out of the murky water to push him back down by the crown of his head. At the end of the dream, he noticed the redneck looked a lot like him.

He was sweating again when he forced his eyes open to see the clock. It was three in the morning, and he felt as if his heart was about to jump out of him. He rolled over and took in a deep breath to calm himself, but the sound of another siren exhaled with him, and then another. He recognized the sound of the last siren. It was the one he'd ordered to be fixed due to the skips in its wail.

He heard four fire trucks. Gator Town had only one, the one with the broken siren. He'd told the city council time and time again that they needed more, but who had listened? Now those other sirens meant that wherever the blaze was, it was big enough for the fire chief to have called the cities of Madison and Perry for more trucks. Hell's bells, he guessed the mayor would have to go see about it all, so C.P. dressed and went to get Fig.

"It ain't my heart," C.P. said when Fig sat up abruptly in bed. "It's all them sirens. Let's go."

"Whatever happened done already happened," Fig said, appearing relieved, and he lay back down. "Ain't nothin' we can do about it now. Anyway, you need to rest."

C.P. kicked over Fig's wooden foot that stood straight up on the floor next to the bed. He snatched off the covers and growled that Fig had better be up and ready to run in two minutes or he'd be the first black man ever buried from Dove's.

"Whoo-whee." Fig grinned. "You gonna integrate the white funeral home just for me, Boss? The Lord might get confused if He sees me sashaying in on the white side."

"Then just tell Him who sent you there," C.P. snapped, shoving the wooden foot with the toe of his boot until it was within Fig's reach. "There's fire burnin' somewheres out yonder and we got to see to it, so strap on that thing!"

They headed downtown in the Jeep, the parched smell of smoke riding with them. At the intersection of Broad and Main, angry neon fingers of orange poked at the dark sky. Framed in the center of the windshield was Porter's Store and Restaurant, surrounded by flames that threatened the entire town.

"Lord, have mercy," Fig said with a sigh.

"Hell's bells!" C.P. shouted, climbing out of the Jeep.

On the sidewalk, he saw Imogene standing in her red bathrobe, like a wad of wrapped sausage, and patting her cheek in rhythm with little squeaking sounds coming from her mouth. When he called to her, she turned and shuffled toward him in enormous fuzzy pink slippers that made soggy sounds as she trudged through the water from fire department hoses. As soon as she reached C.P., she fell into his chest, her hair smelling like the incinerator he ran at his business when he'd thrown in papers—and once, a roll of money—he'd had to dispose of.

"One minute it was here, the next minute, gone!" Imogene sobbed. He put his arms around the bulk of her, rubbing her back as if she was an enormous baby he had to burp. Though he'd never admit it aloud, his heart went out to Imogene, but his head saw more than just Porter's Store and Restaurant burning. He saw the town he controlled, the town he practically created, his town, in jeopardy of becoming nothing but charred ruins.

"Wonder how it happened?" Fig asked.

"Hell if I'm not gonna find out!" C.P. said, unwrapping himself from Imogene in order to locate the fire chief.

C.P. recognized the department head, even under the smoke and hard helmet, by the way the man gave orders, weak ones, like he had no gumption when it came to telling people what to do. "Where's Harper?" he bellowed.

The fire chief cowered. "I called him right off, C.P." He gestured limply toward a group of firefighters holding a heavy hose. "You can ask them if I didn't."

Suddenly, Harper came through the smoke near what was left of Porter's Store. "Looks like arson to me," Harper said, emerging from the thick gray veil. "Of course, it could have been an accident, a lit cigarette or something. What do you think, C.P.?"

The sucking sounds of wet slippers and Imogene's voice calling out to him kept C.P. from answering. "I'm sure it was an accident," Imogene said, breathless, when she reached him again, "but only one person could have been responsible. My new cook's the only one smoked. I told him and told him."

"Damn," C.P. said. "Let them people near a match and they set a fire. Pretty soon they're gonna burn us all out." He caught sight of Fig's disappointed face as he said it, and he tried to redeem himself. "Some of them, anyways." Then he pointed a finger at Chief Harper. "You catch that polecat that's burned up my town. I mean it, Harper!"

He didn't know how the spineless fire chief had done it, C.P. told Sarah Neal the next morning, but that wimp ended up saving most of Gator Town. Sitting soot-faced at the end of a long strip of early sunlight on the kitchen table at the cabin, C.P. continued with details of the fire.

"Imogene thinks her cook's responsible," he said, after he described the last look he had of Porter's, and after he slurped the last of the coffee in his cup and held it out for Sarah Neal to get up and pour him some more.

His grandson sat across from him. He'd been staring hopelessly at his mother. She'd been drinking again. At the mention of Imogene's cook, though, the boy seemed interested.

"You know him, Coleman?"

Sarah Neal clicked her tongue. "Maybe one day some people will learn, C.P.," she said in an I-told-you-so voice, pouring coffee into his cup. She attempted to focus her eyes on him as she set the pot on the table.

Coleman rose and left the room, but Sarah Neal paid no attention. She faced C.P., her arms folded in front of her. "Of course, by then," she said, taking a long sigh to taunt him, "it'll probably be too late to learn."

"Learn what?" he snapped at his daughter-in-law, even though he knew he should ignore her when she'd been drinking.

"Why, nobody—not Imogene, and not even you—can get to the end of the road with an enemy on their back." She paused for his comment, but he was too angry to speak.

"You know why, C.P.?" she went on. "Because that enemy rides high on your shoulders with his hands right over your eyes. He's the only one who can see if the end of the road's going to be a good one or a bad one."

She'd stuck the hook into him again, but he remained quiet while she ripped it through. "See, he'll stay on you, go right on with you, if it's a good day." She sat down at the table and pointed a finger at C.P. "But if he sees you heading for a cliff, the enemy won't tell you. He'll jump off just in time to save himself while you fall, hollering for help all the way down. And sometimes," she nodded toward the double glass doors where Fig could be seen mowing the grass, "the enemy has a dark face."

That was all he could take. He hit the table with his fist, spilling his coffee and staining the white cloth. "Shut up, Sarah Neal!"

She put on a tight, satisfied smile, but even from across the table, and even with her mouth shut, he could smell her acidic breath.

Hadn't Charles Robert been able to do anything at all with her? Where was he anyway? Had he just given up? If Pauly had taken the money C.P. offered him, maybe he would have tried harder. But no, the damn doctor said he'd help Sarah Neal just because he wanted to. Hell, the shrink even said he loved her, but it's money and a little twisting of the arm, not some silly love-mush, that gets the job done. Then he saw Coleman pass by the door, and called him back in.

"I asked you if you knew that fellow Imogene hired."

Coleman looked over at his mother at the sink, holding on to the faucet to keep her balance.

"You met him at the restaurant, Granddaddy. His name's Sarge. He was in the army."

"My God, are they all in the army?" Sarah Neal turned on the water, full force.

C.P. ignored her and stared at Coleman. "Reckon he did it?"

"It had to be him."

Right then C.P. noticed how much Coleman resembled Putt: his height, sand-colored hair, the expression of loss in his eyes. There was new depth in his grandson's voice, too. It was Putt's voice. C.P. closed his eyes to clear his mind. He didn't want to admit it, but in his thinking he often confused Coleman with his son. When that happened, he had to stop whatever he was doing to put himself back on track. Lots of things that cropped up in his mind made him angry, but this was the only thing that frightened him, getting confused like that. It was something he'd never bargained for.

The purr of the lawn mower came near the window, and then stopped. "We out of gas," Fig said, opening the screen door.

"Then go get some more," Sarah Neal snapped, slapping a rag on the counter to scrub it.

C.P. reached into his back pocket for the keys to the Jeep and gave them to Fig with a five-dollar bill. Then he turned to his grandson. "Go with him, Coleman. And go by Imogene's, too. Tell her not to worry. I'll take care of everythin'."

"Mr. C. P. Bridgeman," Sarah Neal slurred in rhythm with the push of the rag, "takes care of everything. He thinks he's God Almighty."

C.P. watched through the screen as Coleman and Fig left. Sarah Neal was wrong. Fig was not on his back, but at his right hand. "The mayor's Right-Hand Man" was what people called Fig, but he was much more than that. C.P. couldn't let on to anybody, certainly not to Sarah Neal, that Fig was his first-born son, the product of a drunken dare in his younger years with Aggie. That was before Emma came along. She'd taken Fig in without knowing the truth after her husband made up a salable story about getting tired of seeing a little colored boy, old enough to work, hanging around his Gator Town business doing nothing.

He hired Fig to help him poach the rivers and feed the catch, then he made Fig part of the act, entertaining the Yankees who came to see Florida. C.P. would prop a stick between the jaws of Uncle Al, the biggest gator he had, and then have Fig poke his foot between Uncle Al's giant teeth. The Yankees loved it, until one day the stick broke just as Emma was bringing her husband his lunch. She was horrified.

She threw the bloody boy into her 1930 Ford and rushed him to the hospital, then stayed there with him. When the hospital said he could go, Emma brought him home with her. She made C.P. cut down a young live oak and make part of the trunk into a wooden foot for Fig. From the rest of the tree, she talked C.P. into making a few pieces of furniture for the back bedroom of their first house in town and put Fig there, until Putt was born. Later, after the Bridgemans came up in the world and moved to the inlet, Emma had C.P. build the fish house and installed Fig in it, along with the furniture and her entire set of *The Book of Knowledge,* from which she taught him to read. For each of Fig's growing years, Emma saw to it that a new wooden foot was made to fit him.

C.P. was sorry he hadn't been honest with Emma, but thinking of Fig made him smile. What people would say about C. P. Bridgeman if they knew! Fig wouldn't smile about it, though. Fig would look serious, say something like "Some people can't smell nothin' but rotten, even if it's a rose stuck under their nose." He knew Fig would say something like that, because he knew Fig loved him.

With his thought of love, his mind moved back to Emma. He'd truly adored the woman. Yet somewhere along the way he lost her. Because of what? Some itch he had to scratch? Hell, he couldn't think about it. If he did, he'd have to remember the look on his sweet Emma's face after he came from the woman who was Eloise's mother. He'd told Emma it was only a lunch, but she'd smelled the suntan oil and a little more than tuna fish on his breath.

He didn't want to remember her disillusioned expression, or the gradual shrinking of Emma's heart to a fist-sized knot, watching it grow smaller and tighter and more silent, until it stopped beating altogether. Hell, if he ever thought he was God Almighty, like Sarah Neal said, he wouldn't have let his sweet Emma die like that, with Fig, not him, at her side. Fig told him time and again that Emma had forgiven all his transgressions. Once he told him something stranger. With her last breath, Emma said that because of Jesus's mercy, and not hers, she would see C.P. in heaven.

Of course the part about heaven was hogwash. Oh, he knew that some day he would die too, because all roads come to an end. But there was nothing spectacular waiting like Emma thought, or like Sarah Neal prayed for. People just vanished when the road ran out. Maybe they simply fell off the edge of the cliff Sarah Neal always prattled about and then disappeared to some black nothing. It might be a shame there wasn't anything in the dark to catch him when it was his time to fall, but there just wasn't. Because there wasn't, all that mattered was what he could actually do with whoever and whatever was left in the short road ahead of him.

"C.P.!" Sarah Neal was yelling his name. "Are you deaf?" By the time he noticed her, she was right up in his face, bent over the table, her crucifx and silver medal clicking together in the air between them. "All right, just sit there like a bump in the road." She grabbed her Dixie cup from the counter and left the kitchen, the whiskey splashing over the brim and spotting the floor.

Oh yes, the road. The short road ahead of him. Fig was on the road with him, but who else? He thought first of Imogene. Was she with him? No longer as a lover, but as a friend he provided for? He'd warned her about trusting strangers off the street. And Coleman? He was like Putt warmed over, except for the metal plate that had kept Putt in a constant war. Inside Coleman, though, there was a battle going on too, maybe not as noticeable as in Putt but a battle nonetheless. C.P. knew the signs. That's why he would continue to teach Coleman how to win that war. And Coleman would be victorious, he thought with pride, because one part of that boy was just like him. Then there was Sarah Neal, the major bump in his road, that little snake of a woman, always coiled in front of his every step, hissing out his misdeeds through a haze of alcohol.

All of them depended on him. In fact the whole of Gator Town relied on him, and it wasn't his nature to let things get out of hand. He would keep going. There was plenty of time left on the road ahead of C.P. Bridgeman.

After Fig filled the Jeep with gas, and he and Coleman gave C.P.'s message of hope to Imogene, who cried and sniffled that C.P. was a piece of pure white saving grace, and after they said good-bye to her and Fig made a point of telling Coleman that grace doesn't always come in white, he and Coleman went back to the cabin.

The boss was waiting on the steps, unwrapping the tape around the hook on his cane pole, ready to take the boy fishing. He gave Fig a wink. "Me and Coleman's got more to do than monkey business. We got fish to catch."

Fig watched them get into the boat and head out into the inlet, then he went to the fish house. He was lying on his bed, reading a volume of *The Book of Knowledge,* when the door opened.

Clayton Jackson eased in, wearing an army shirt with what looked like a tobacco knife stuck in his belt.

"Well, howdy-do, brother," Clayton said, grinning.

Fig lowered the book. "Never been a brother of yours."

"Oh yeah? Well, you know who I am."

"You're the one with the hungry look, the one I don't want to know."

"But you recognize me, don't you? We come from the same old auntie. Me the old black sheep and you the creamy half and half." He began to poke around the fish house, fingering things, until he stopped in front of the crucifix.

"You ever get yourself saved?" Fig asked.

"Once. Don't reckon it took, though." He picked up *The Book of Knowledge* from Fig's lap. "You know how to read this?"

"A sweet white lady taught me."

"Mama Nem? She the only time I seen sweet and white together. She should have took me instead of you to eat at her rich white dinner table." Clayton handed the book back to Fig. "I reckon she felt sorry for you, one foot and all. And of course you are kinda of related to her husband, huh? You're lucky he didn't cut off more than your foot."

Fig rose from the bed and stood face-to-face with Clayton. "That was an accident. Are you the one burned down Miz Imogene's place?"

"That was an accident too, brother."

"They gonna find you."

"No, they ain't. My luck's changed. Took me some years, but I got to the table." He nodded in the direction of the Bridgeman's house. "That little-bitty white lady up there and her tall honky child? I been in their house. I ate plenty. She don't never lock the door. I let myself in anytime I want to."

"You're lying."

"I ain't lyin' brother. I know where they sleep."

Fig grabbed him by the throat. "What you after, Clayton?"

"That Jeep up yonder. You got the key, don't you?"

"It ain't nothin' I'll give to the likes of you."

Clayton pulled the knife from his belt and pointed it at Fig. "Brother, I believe you gonna have to."

Out on the inlet, C.P. pulled in a crappie. "Whoo-whee! Seven up on you, Coleman, and you ain't caught one." He stepped on the fish to take the hook from its mouth. "You remember what I told you now," he said, holding up the rusty hook. "This here's the key. Hook 'em while you can." Suddenly he grabbed at his chest.

"What's wrong, Granddaddy?" His grandfather looked unusually pale.

"Indigestion, I reckon. Hand me that can of crawlers. Somebody out here's got to catch somethin'."

The red sun was just over the tree-line and the cicadas were strumming out time for dusk when Coleman's grandfather threw out his line. Then, without a sound, C.P. Bridgeman clutched his chest and fell forward over the side of the boat. His B.O.S.S. hat fell in first, and then his body descended like an anchor into the deep, dark water.

Coleman dived overboard, churning the murkiness groping for C.P., but it was several minutes before his hands found the old man's hand. He pulled his grandfather close and in the flash of that tragic moment he realized how much he loved him.

As they neared the surface, the lighter water exposed his grandfather's face. It was stricken with disbelief, as if all he'd ever thought to be true was a lie. When they broke through to the air, his grandfather's slate-gray eyes glared at him, and Coleman was sure he heard the old man say, "Don't ever let 'em nail you to the cross, boy. Hook 'em first!"

Later, looking at C.P. in the open casket, he would doubt he heard those words at all.

Clayton Jackson, the knife in his hand, stood eye to eye with Fig. "I need the key, brother, and I expect you'll give it to me. See, I got tired of eatin' here and livin' in a briar patch. Got to get on down the road and—." The sound of the boat pulling into the slip and Coleman's mournful cry, "Fig!" stopped whatever else he was going to say.

Fig grabbed *The Book of Knowledge,* knocked the knife from Clayton's grasp, and then held the weapon to the man's throat. "This better be the last time I see you, Clayton Jackson. Now get! I ain't got time to talk no more!" He slapped the knife on the bookcase and hurried out to the dock.

14

From the dock, Fig carried C.P.'s body like a baby in his arms, up the lawn and toward the driveway, where Chief Harper and two young black men waited in the glare of the bleeding red light of an ambulance. Coleman walked behind, with Sarah Neal beside him holding a blanket around the shoulders of her son.

"Coleman, I know what you're feeling," she said, her breath burning his face. "I don't want you to blame yourself. You did everything you could do."

"You don't know what I'm feeling."

"But I do! For years, I've felt guilty about your father's death."

"I don't feel guilty. I didn't kill anybody. You did."

His mother stopped at once. Her hand dropped away from his shoulders, and the blanket she was holding fell behind him on the grass.

Ahead, Fig spoke back and forth in two voices. "Now, look what you gone and done to yourself, Boss. Who gonna be up there to take care of you?"

The other voice replied. "He gonna be with the angels, Fig, singin' with them. And he's gonna be with sweet Mama Nem and Putt, too. He gonna be tellin' them all what to do."

"Well, he does know how to boss," Fig responded to himself. "But he ain't gonna fit in with no angels."

When Fig approached the ambulance, two young black drivers with their heads stuck together like double acorns whispered to each other.

"Just look at that sucker, carryin' the mayor so sweetlike, even after the old man cut off his foot so he couldn't get away."

"You ain't got it right," the other man said. "I heard the mayor was Fig's own daddy."

Coleman came up beside them. "Shut your damn mouths and put him in the ambulance!" Inside his head, he heard C.P.'s voice: "Attaboy!"

The chief put a hand on Coleman's shoulder, then he said to the drivers, "Take him to Dove's, and tell them I said to lay him out nice. C. P. Bridgeman wasn't perfect, but he wasn't quite the devil neither."

The night after C.P. drowned, Sarah Neal ran out of whiskey again. She didn't want to go get more, but she wanted more. She thought of Charles Robert and how she missed him, wondering if he had cooled off enough to help her out. He would know she was under stress with C.P.'s death. Maybe he would relent and buy the whiskey for her. She dialed his number.

He answered with a sleepy hello, but she couldn't make herself speak.

"Sarah Neal, is that you? You know I love you with all my heart, but if you're drinking, I don't want to talk to you."

She slammed down the receiver. It was too much of an ultimatum: him or the bottle. She needed it only to get through C.P.'s funeral. Then afterward, she'd quit. "This will be the last time," she said to the empty room.

In the driveway, she raised the top on the Bel Air because she thought it might rain, then she drove downtown to the liquor store. By the time she came out and was getting back into the car, it was raining so hard she almost slipped on the wet sidewalk. She could barely see the road.

The brown bag lay beside her, calling to her seductively. She pulled out the bottle and took a long drink, pressing her foot on the accelerator because she wanted to get to the cabin quickly. Suddenly, the car skidded sideways, into the path of an oncoming truck. She twisted the wheel to avoid a collision and rammed into a telephone pole on the side of the road. It was the last thing she remembered until she came to. She couldn't get the door open then, and was crawling out of the window when she saw the blue lights of a police car approaching.

Chief Harper recognized the car and hurried over. "Sarah Neal? Are you all right?" He put out a hand to help.

She couldn't let him near her. He might smell whiskey on her breath. "I'm fine," she said, shoving his hand away. "Just take me home."

"Better take you to the hospital first."

"No, I'm fine!"

"Well, I'll have to call a wrecker," he said, and walked back to his patrol car to get on the radio. "Margaret? . . . No, I ain't found the arsonist yet. I want you to call Dr. Pauly and tell him Sarah Neal Bridgeman's had a little accident out here on Winton Road, then call Beave's Wrecker Service."

The bent Bel Air was being hooked to the wrecker truck when Charles Robert drove up.

"My God, Sarah Neal, what happened?" He put an arm around her, and then drew back quickly. "Put her in the drunk tank, chief," he said to Harper. "It's what she's chosen."

"Don't you dare!" she hollered at Harper.

"When are you going to learn?" Charles Robert asked. "You've got a son who needs you, a man who loves you, and a life you could make something out of, and all you want is the booze." He started for his car.

She ran after him. "Don't leave me, Charles Robert. I do want you, and I want Coleman. I intend to quit. I will quit."

He put his hands firmly on her shoulders. "Say it again, and mean it."

"I love you and my son, not the whiskey. I do mean it. This time, I do!"

She knew that was what he wanted her to say, but in her heart, she believed it was true.

The whole day before his grandfather's funeral, Coleman relived the drowning. "If only I'd gotten to him quicker," he said to Fig as they stood in the kitchen, "maybe he wouldn't have died."

"Did you tell that to your mama?" Fig was holding the B.O.S.S. hat in his hands, and his eyes were puffy and red.

"No! Why would I?"

"She understands all about guilt."

"It's not the same."

Fig looked straight at him. "Ain't it? You're wieldin' an awful sharp knife, honey boy. Look out you don't cut yourself with it."

He wanted to say something smart, but Fig was hurting too.

Coleman watched him go through the living room with the hat still in his hand and out onto the porch. Fig stood there awhile, as if wondering where to go next. Then he walked down the yard to the fish house. Coleman thought Fig a fool for putting up with C.P., but he never questioned Fig's love for the old man, or his grandfather's often disguised affection for Fig.

"Coleman?"

He turned to find Anna at the screen door.

"I'm sorry about your grandfather," she said as he let her in. "I know you tried to save him. You were very heroic."

But the word *tried* made him uncomfortable. And heroic? "My grandfather's still dead," he said brusquely.

"Do you remember the present I wanted to give you?" she asked, ignoring his rudeness.

He nodded.

"I'd like to give it to you now. Will you come with me?"

He followed her to the red tips and sat beside her on the fallen leaves. This time, he told himself, he wouldn't run away.

From the pocket of her dress, she drew a small statue that glowed bluish white in the palm of her hand. She offered it to him, but he only stared at it.

"It's Jesus's mother."

He knew that. He was unraveling a statement his mother made years before: "A little statue of the Virgin Mary next to your father's heart when he was wounded."

"She's phosphorescent. I put her under the lamp light all night so she would shine enough for you to see."

"Where did you find her?"

"In the patch between our houses, on the day I scratched myself cleaning up after that tramp. Maybe she was his, but I saved her for you."

The ghostly light illuminated the tips of his fingers as she put the statue into his hand.

"She's called Our Lady of Hope," Anna said, watching him closely. "My mother used to say that the most beautiful gift in this world is hope, because it comes directly from God."

He fiddled with the little statue until it became warm in his hand, remembering the night his father stirred the dark water of the inlet into stars. Like Anna, his father had likened the stirring to the gift of hope. Coleman didn't want to appear fragile enough to need it, though, so he handed the statue back to her.

She looked disappointed, even annoyed. "Why can't you accept a gift? What are you afraid of?"

"I'm not afraid," he said. "I just don't need it."

Anna didn't speak for what seemed an eternity. Then she dug a hole in the earth with her fingers. She set the base of the statue in it, patted the soil around it, then dusted off her hands. "Everyone needs hope to live in this world. Now you'll know where to find it."

Once, she'd told him that this place beneath the red tips was their special place where they could say whatever they wanted to say. He hadn't wanted to say anything then. Now he seemed unable to keep from talking. "My father was crazy, and my mother shot him for that. The newspaper said it was an accident, but I'm sure my mother did it."

"You saw her shoot him?"

"I saw her with the gun in her hand."

"Maybe she didn't."

He always blamed his mother, but now, as he recalled that awful night, it struck him for the first time that his father may have killed himself. No, that wasn't true. It couldn't be.

"She killed him," Coleman said with finality. "And now my grandfather's dead too. My mother's the only one left, and she's a damn drunk!"

Coleman did just what he didn't want to do: appear vulnerable and weak to Anna. After all, as his mother said, she was a Saylor, and the Saylors were enemies. He had to draw some weapon from within to fight the adversary she might become. "I could be as crazy as my daddy," he said, trying to look sinister.

Anna only laughed. "You're not crazy, Coleman. Your daddy wasn't crazy either. Fig said he wasn't."

"And what did Fig say about my mother?"

"That she loved your father, and that she loves and needs you."

"That's not true."

"It is true. All you have to do is reach out for her. Love will reach back. Love always reaches back."

He didn't call her an idealist. He didn't tell Anna that she was a dreamer who saw goodness instead of evil. He didn't say anything like that, because as soon as the word *love* left her lips, it rushed into his head and he couldn't push it out. What he finally said was "I love you, Anna." Then he was unable to keep from kissing her.

"I love you too, Coleman." And she kissed him back.

His mother promised she wouldn't drink before the funeral. As far as Coleman could tell, she hadn't, all due to Charles Robert, the only one able to reason with her. Afterward, Sarah Neal insisted that Coleman ride back to the cabin with them. Fig followed in the Jeep, but when he arrived, he wouldn't get out. Coleman pleaded with him to come into the house, but he only sat there, singing softly, over and over:

> *Let us break bread together on our knees.*
> *When I fall on my knees, with my face to*
> *the rising sun, oh Lord, have mercy on me.*

Inside, Coleman, his mother, and Charles Robert picked at the offerings of funeral food that lined the counter while the song floated through the screen door. Finally, Sarah Neal had enough.

"God, he's driving me crazy!" She stomped down the steps and stood beside the window of the Jeep, as if Fig was her disobedient child.

"Good grief, Fig, you act as if he was Jesus Christ. All that man did for you was to keep you from walking on two good feet."

"Well, he always give me somewhere to limp to. Ain't got nowhere to go now."

For several minutes, there was only the sound of the crickets. Then Sarah Neal threw up her hands. "For heaven's sake! You'll stay right here, so come on in and break your darned old bread with us."

Charles Robert stood waiting for her in the threshold of the door. "Sweet Jesus," she said, coming toward him. "Is there anybody in Gator Town that's got good sense?"

He kissed her on her cheek. "I know one person."

Coleman's mother smiled at her shrink, and he smiled back at her. Then she hollered at Fig again. "I said come in here and eat, and I mean right now!" Fig came.

Late in the afternoon the day after his grandfather's funeral, Sarah Neal was more than fidgety. She hadn't had a drink in several days and she didn't seem to know what to do with herself. She'd called Charles Robert four times already, and after every conversation with him, she seemed to calm down a little. Now the enemy behind the cabinet door seemed to fire at her again. "Just get through today," she kept repeating.

He was surprised that his mother appeared to be in such agony, almost like a wounded soldier lying on a battleground held by the enemy. His heart told him to reach for her, but his mind said she was getting what she deserved.

When she wasn't staring at the cabinet, Sarah Neal wouldn't

let Coleman out of her sight. She went into events long past and brought up his daddy and what he'd been like before Coleman knew him, before his head was emptied of all that Sarah Neal thought should have been in it. Then she lashed into his grandfather. Yet beneath her tirade, Coleman perceived a telling ache for the man she believed to be her antagonist. Finally, she worked herself up into such a stew that she lay down on top of Mama Nem's patterned quilt and fell asleep.

Coleman rode his bike to their special place, thinking Anna might be there. Only Our Lady of Hope shined beneath the branches.

He decided to go back home, maybe even talk to his mother if she was awake. When he went through the patch, he noticed a pile of old cans, food wrappers, and an empty carton of Camel cigarettes. Anna said she'd cleaned up the patch, but maybe she hadn't seen all this.

Over at the Saylors' house, the usual station wagon was gone, replaced by a red sports car. He went up to the house to find Anna and saw the front door standing ajar. From inside, he heard a female voice, so he went in.

The voice wasn't Anna's. Facing the living room window, with her back toward him, was a red-haired woman. She was twisting the telephone cord in her fingers as she spoke into the receiver. "C.P. may be dead, Harper, but if little Miss Sarah Neal was to find out the part you played in that old rape charge I made against her husband, it'd be no more police chief for you."

As the woman turned in his direction, he recognized her, and he backed into a corner. Whatever Eloise Saylor had to say he intended to hear.

"Look, Harper, maybe I did the dirty work, but you cooked it up. And my split wasn't enough. You gave me only half of that fifty thousand you hooked old C.P. for, and it didn't stretch over five years in Chicago. I need at least twenty-five more."

Granddaddy got hooked? If Coleman hadn't been so furious, he might have seen the humor in that.

"Oh yes, you've got it," Eloise went on. "Don't forget you and I spent a lot of quality time together. I know what you're into."

Coleman began to join the pieces. Chief Harper, his grandfather's business partner and so-called friend for thirty years, had betrayed him with this woman. Even worse, if Eloise hadn't been involved, his mother might not have shot his father. His enemy stood right in front of him. He wouldn't let her get away! He walked toward her.

Eloise was smiling into the phone. "Oh, why don't you just come on over? I won't be playin' nursemaid all night. The kid'll be going beddy-bye and we can have some fun."

Then she saw Coleman. "Chief, I'll call you back."

She set down the telephone and came toward him, extending her arms as if for a hug. "Well, for goodness 'sake, is that little Coleman Bridgeman all grown up to become such a good-lookin' man?"

"You lied about my father. He never raped you."

She looked startled at first. "Now Coleman," she said, "that was such a long time ago. And your daddy? Well, you just have to forgive him. You know he wasn't right in the head."

"You and Chief Harper made it all up, to bribe Granddaddy."

She moved in closer. "You know how men are. You're almost a man. Why, I wouldn't be surprised if you were thinkin' about me just like your crazy handsome daddy did." She was right up on him, reaching out to brush his sleeve with her fingers.

He knocked her hand away. "Granddaddy always said you were nothing but trash."

From behind him came a cry, like a child in pain, and he knew

Anna had heard everything.

She ran from the house. He followed, calling out her name, but she didn't stop until she reached their special place. She was on her knees, next to the little statue, when he reached her.

"I'm sorry for what Aunt Eloise did to your father. It was evil." He knelt beside her. "It wasn't your fault."

"But I believed her. I thought your daddy raped her. I even felt sorry for her."

"Sometimes it's those you least expect that end up licking your bones. It's just not a sweet world." They were his grandfather's words.

"But why isn't it?"

He touched her hand. "Because the people you love are the ones who hurt you most."

She looked up at him with a pure and simple innocence, the same as when she told him to reach out for love. Do that and you might get crucified, he thought. Hadn't she heard of what happened to Jesus?

"I'll never hurt you, Coleman."

He noticed the statue, still glowing. It looked insignificant, yet it stirred something inside him. Even if, one day, she did hurt him, he thought he could live through the pain.

Anna touched his face and moved into his arms, next to his heart.

When he reached the cabin again, a note from his mother was attached to the screen: "Coleman, Gone to dinner with Charles Robert. Plenty of funeral food left in fridge. P.S. Fig is in the fish house. He won't stay at C.P.'s alone anymore. Guess he's here for good."

He pulled off the note and went inside. He opened the refrigerator to a rush of cool air and took out a bottle of milk that was pushed behind a half-eaten casserole. Stuck to the side of it was another note, from Mrs. Porter this time: "Ain't nobody gonna miss him like I will, but God bless y'all anyways."

He took a swig of milk from the bottle, put it back, and heard the sliding glass door opening. "Fig?" he called, and went into the living room.

It was Sarge who stood there, grinning. "Got some people huntin' for me, honky child."

"They ought to string you up by your toenails for burning down an old lady's store." He noticed a knife stuck in Sarge's belt.

"Wasn't me done it."

"Hell, I know it was you."

"You wrong, honky child. All they wants me for is because I'm black. Can't help it if the store burn up. I didn't steal no money." Sarge reached into the pocket of the old army shirt, took out a pack of Camels, and lit one like he meant to stay awhile.

"How did you know where I lived?"

"I been knowin' that a long time, honky child, and I thank you and your mama for feedin' me so well."

"Feeding you?"

Sarge gave an arrogant smile. "Reckon I been eatin' at this house for some time now. I stay just close enough to take what I want and leave what I don't. You might call that evil, honky child, but ain't none of y'all seen fit to lock the door on it."

He remembered the nights when he'd heard someone in the kitchen. It must have been Sarge. He was the tramp who left garbage in the patch—and the statue Anna found when she was cleaning up.

Sarge blew a stream of smoke into the air that hovered around the sofa. He followed the haze with his eyes until it disintegrated just above the end table and the small framed wedding picture of Sarah Neal and Putt. He picked up the photograph and held it close to his face. "I remember the first time I seen this picture."

"You've been in this room too?" The thought of it galled Coleman.

"I never said I been in this particular room, honky child. I just said I seen the picture before."

"Then where did you see it?"

As soon as he asked the question, he remembered what his mother had said, years ago, in this same room: "Before he left, I gave your daddy two things: this picture and a little statue of the Blessed Virgin Mary that glowed in the dark."

"You were the man my father saved in the Pacific!" he shouted to Sarge.

Sarge put down the picture, as if to to make some disclosure. Then the screen door slammed, and Coleman heard his mother's voice.

"Coleman? Where are you? Did you eat?"

Sarge looked surprised and snatched the knife from his belt. "Better be quiet, honky child."

Coleman lunged for Sarge. The knife flew up between them, cutting a shallow slash in Coleman's forearm. Sarge seemed shocked, even sorry.

"My God!" Sarah Neal said when she entered the room and saw the blood on Coleman's arm. "Who are you, and what do you think you're doing to my son?"

Sarge backed his way around the dining room table, pointing the knife at her. "Y'all better stay away else you gonna get hurt some more."

Still, she went forward until she had pressed him against the wall. His shadow loomed high above him, showing him small.

"Who is this, Coleman?" His mother was livid, but even better, she was stone sober.

"It's the man Daddy saved."

She ran her eyes like claws over Sarge's face. "This is the man your father saved?"

"He knew the picture. It has to be him."

"I don't know nothin' about any savin'. Only man ever saved me is Jesus." Sarge raised his eyes to the ceiling. "Except right now Jesus don't seem to be doin' his job so good."

Ignoring the knife, she poked a stiff finger into his chest. "You will not dispute the wisdom of Jesus in my house!" Then his mother turned abruptly and hurried down the hall.

Sarge appeared staggered. "Lady, get back here now!"

From the bedroom came the sound of bureau drawers opening and closing.

Sarge headed for the sliding glass door, but Coleman blocked him. "Give me the knife, Sarge," Coleman said, reaching for it.

"I ain't! Now you get away, or you gonna get cut again." Then his attention went back to the noise of the drawers. "Lady, what are you doin' in there? I got your son. I can cut his throat if I want to." His eyes moved like little black marbles rolling back and forth from Coleman to the clicking sound of heels coming back down the hall.

There was hatred and maybe a little fear in his mother's eyes when she reentered the room. In her hand was his father's gun, the barrel pointed at Sarge.

"Now I'll take back what you took from me," she said, moving toward him until he was again trapped against the wall.

Sarge wiggled the knife at her, his voice quivering. "I only took a little food, only a little bit of food. Nothin' you'd have missed."

Her eyes narrowed. "You bastard. You took my heart and soul.

You took everything I had."

His mother faced her target, feet apart, shoulders squared, her arms straight out and locked. Coleman was sure she meant to shoot him dead.

"Jesus, save me," Sarge pleaded, his eyes to the ceiling. "Just once more!"

"Nobody's going to save you this time." Sarah Neal took in a breath and began to gently squeeze the trigger in a steady caress.

A voice came from behind her. "That gonna satisfy your heart once and for all, Miz Sarah Neal?"

His mother didn't turn. "Leave me alone, Fig."

"Oh, I'm gonna leave you alone. That's the enemy you been hatin' for so long. That's the man Putt saved. So you go and kill him."

Coleman couldn't believe the words were coming from Fig, of all people.

Sarge looked gray as ashes. "Hey, brother," he said to Fig. "Tell her to let me go. I'll give you that old lady's fifteen dollars. That's all it was: fifteen dollars in that cash register. You can have it all."

Fig just stood there.

"It wasn't my fault," Sarge whined. "I ain't nothin' but a poor black man that's had hard times. I'm just like you, ain't I? People always out to get us."

Fig moved beside Sarah Neal. "You're not like me. I ain't made a lifetime out of being a victim."

The man turned back to Sarah Neal. "It was an accident. Don't kill me, lady. I swear on my aunt Aggie's boneyard. It was an accident!"

Sarah Neal looked at Coleman. "I want the truth. Is this the man your daddy saved?"

"He knew the picture."

"Oh, he's the one, all right," Fig said. "If you're gonna shoot him, then shoot him now."

"What are you trying to do?" Coleman asked.

"She wants the truth, don't she?" Fig said coldly. "Kill him, Miz Sarah Neal."

She set her eyes on the looming shadow on her wall until her fingers began to tremble. Then she lowered her arms, the gun dangling in her right hand. "I can't."

Coleman thought Fig let out a long breath, but it might have been his own that he heard. Sarge gave a loud, "Praise you, Lord Jesus!"

"Get out of here!" his mother commanded.

Sarge headed for the door, then turned with a menacing look and thrust the knife through the air like an imaginative child playing war. "Y'all better not tell nobody you seen me." And he was gone.

Sarah Neal stared at the shut door for a moment. Then she burst into laughter. "Surely that wasn't the man Putt saved. That childish fool?"

"I think he was," Coleman said.

"Don't matter if it was him or not," Fig said. "If Miz Sarah Neal couldn't kill somebody she hate, she couldn't kill nobody. She too sweet a white lady for that."

His mother set her eyes on Fig like she'd never seen anyone she loved more.

———

Dear Coleman,

By the time you get this, I will be on my way home.
Aunt Eloise felt it was not in her best interest to stay in
Gator Town. After she takes me back to Birmingham,
she will search for new opportunities in another place.
I don't know how I will stand the ride with her after
what she did. You keep the statue. Remember me when
you look at it. I'll write soon.

Love,
Anna

P.S. Fig said he'd look after the kittens.

In the place Anna called special, he read the note again, then crumbled it in his hand. She was gone, taking so much of him with her that he felt empty. Only the tiny statue remained within his reach. He took it up and put it into his pocket. Anna said she'd never hurt him, but she did.

"I can't find Fig anywhere." Charles Robert pulled back a chair and sat on the other side of Coleman and Sarah Neal at the conference table, in the room where Mr. Alfred Baldwin, Esquire, was to read C.P.'s will. "He's not at the cabin, the fish house, or C.P.'s house in town. We'll just have to go on without him."

"Granddaddy would have wanted him here," Coleman said.

"Well, if he's not here, he's not here," his mother said, as if impatient to hear what had been in C.P.'s head.

Mr. Baldwin, a squarely built man in round glasses, spoke to Charles Robert. "C.P. made you the executor of his will."

Charles Robert looked surprised. "Why would he do that and

not tell me?"

"The mayor said he knew you wouldn't refuse, so he saw no reason to ask you, Dr. Pauly."

Sarah Neal brushed a hand through the air. "That was typical of C.P."

"He was right, though," Charles Robert said. "I wouldn't have said no."

C.P.'s lawyer nodded, aligning his papers at the end of the table. Then Imogene Porter bustled through the door.

His mother seemed caught off guard. "Imogene?"

"Don't ask me why, child," Mrs. Porter said, fanning her moist face with a handkerchief. "Mr. Baldwin told me to come, and to tell you the truth, baby, I'm afraid of what I'm gonna hear."

Mr. Baldwin cleared his throat. "Let's just read the will. 'I, Cleveland Puttman Bridgeman, being of sound mind—.'"

"Now, that's debateable," Sarah Neal remarked, but Mr. Baldwin went on reading.

After a few minutes, every face at the table had a wide-eyed expression: "'These and all other properties, numbering forty-seven parcels in all, I bequeath to my grandson, Coleman, to be held in trust by my executor, Dr. Charles Robert Pauly, until Coleman's twenty-first birthday. In addition, besides the fishing advice I've already given him, I bequeath to my grandson the sum of four hundred and fifty thousand dollars, also to be held in trust, with the exception of the cost of tuition to St. Benedict Preparatory Academy and College. This tuition will be paid out over the next six years until Coleman has graduated, then he must come home to Gator Town and run my business.'"

Coleman shook his head slowly, amazed. "Still baiting the hook, Granddaddy?"

"My God, he sure caught a lot with it," Sarah Neal said. "And

St. Benedict? A Catholic school? I don't believe it!"

Mr. Baldwin pushed up his glasses. "May I go on?"

Sarah Neal gave a nod of approval.

"'To Miz Imogene Porter—.'"

"Oh Lordy." Mrs. Porter wiped under each eye with the hand-kerchief.

"'—who never let me forget I was young once, I bequeath the deed to the property and what's left of Porter's Store and Restaurant, along with the sum of fifty thousand dollars to build it back again.'"

"Oh, that man," Mrs. Porter bawled. "That sweet, sweet man. Now y'all know whose store it really was, and he never told nobody!" She gave one last "Oh Lordy" before her false teeth fell out. She caught them in her handkerchief.

Coleman gave a quiet laugh. "So, I've been working for Granddaddy."

"Is there anybody that man didn't own?" his mother asked.

Mr. Baldwin turned pointedly to Sarah Neal. "'To my daughter-in-law, Sarah Neal Bridgeman, I bequeath the cabin, which she already calls her house anyway. But let her know that she has to keep Fig on to do the yard work, because I don't want it to go to pot, and Sarah Neal would let it.'"

"A person can't do everything. If he wants Fig, fine."

"I'm not finished, Sarah Neal," Mr. Baldwin said. He continued. "'If she accepts the cabin, Sarah Neal must also accept a marriage proposal from Dr. Charles Robert Pauly, who will give her some of that peace and happiness she's been looking down a bottle neck to find.'"

Charles Robert smiled, and Sarah Neal was finally struck dumb.

"This last section is for Fig. We'll go ahead with it, even

though he's not present."

"Y'all lookin' for me?" Fig peeped around the door and limped in. He looked a little fatter around the waist. "Well, I'm here."

When he eased into an old wooden rocker against the wall, the front of his plaid shirt began to pulsate. A pair of round eyes peeked out from between the buttons, then the furry face of a kitten, followed by another pair of eyes and more kittens. One by one, Fig stuffed the heads back inside, patted his chest, and crossed his wooden foot over his real one. "Y'all go on ahead now."

Mr. Baldwin sighed. "'To Fig, I bequeath three things: First, I leave him my house in town, but he'll have to sell it because we all know what the neighbors would say if he lived there without me. Whatever he gets for it is his. Second, I leave him the Jeep, so he don't need no feet to get him where he's going. And third, I leave him my cap. Fig thinks he's the boss anyway.'"

Fig gave Coleman a wink, pulled the B.O.S.S. cap from the waist of his blue jeans, and slapped it on his head.

"And that's about all," Mr. Baldwin said, letting out a happy breath. "Oh, except for this right here, hand written by the mayor a couple of days before he died. It says: 'I reckon y'all got what your hearts was hungry for. If you didn't, change your bait and throw out your line again. Don't never give up hope! C. P. Bridgeman.'"

On Coleman's sixteenth birthday, Sarah Neal married Charles Robert in St. Michael's Catholic Church. The reception was in the church hall and Sarah Neal had the cake made with birthday candles on one side and wedding bells on the other. That night, after she threw out all her whiskey bottles, Charles Robert moved into the cabin.

A few days later, at dawn, Coleman stood on the porch, his eyes wandering between the circle his father had made and the vacant Saylors' house. There wasn't much left of the circle now, just as there was nothing left of Anna.

Once again he thought of the gifts his father and Anna had shown him: that one hand can stir beauty into the dark water, that one hopeful touch offers the possibility of love. The inlet, with its secret stars, was still there. And the small statue was still in his pocket.

He heard his mother come up behind and felt her hesitation as she stood beside him.

"You're up early," he said.

"It's easier when you're sober."

"You haven't been drinking?" It was more an accusation than a question.

"Not lately. Well, not much." She touched his chin and turned it toward hers. "Let's just say I'm trying. Can you try too, Coleman?"

"Try what?"

"To forgive me."

"If you didn't shoot Daddy, then did he—?"

"It was an accident," she said quickly. Then she fingered the crucifix around her neck. "Your daddy was who he was. And I loved him. It was the unhappy situation I couldn't love."

Every instance was always about her. Had she ever thought about him? He was suddenly tired of confronting her, though. "It must have been hard for you."

Her face brightened. "No doubt it was hard for you too," she said unexpectedly. "Even hard for C.P. In his way. That old goat loved all of us."

"He twisted a few arms, but Eloise still got the better of him." He realized he shouldn't have mentioned their former neighbor.

"Eloise?"

"Never mind. She's gone. And Anna's gone," he said, and he took the statue from his pocket. "She gave me this."

"Our Lady of Hope!" His mother brushed a finger over it. "It looks exactly like the one I gave your father before he left for the war. There were probably thousands of these little statues back then. We tried to send hope with our loved ones."

Coleman was afraid she would start up again about his father. Instead she paused, and then asked, "Where did she get it?"

"She found it in the sand."

His mother touched his shoulder. "I was wrong about Anna. You'll see. She'll be back. I'm sure of it, Coleman." She laughed. "But she'd better not bring Eloise with her!"

He loved the sound of her laugh, but maybe she was letting Eloise off the hook. He wasn't sure he could do that. There were people in this world who couldn't be trusted, and Eloise was one of them, an enemy. Once he thought of his mother as an enemy too.

"I do love you, Coleman," she said.

He looked down the yard to the circle. The tangled scrub rose against a tender, brightening sky, and a crane foraged to satisfy its hunger. He turned to his mother. She opened her hand. Coleman rested his hand within it.

About
the Author

Kaye Park Hinckley earned a bachelor's degree in fine arts from Spring Hill College, in Mobile, Alabama. A former advertising agency owner, her fiction has appeared in several literary journals, including *Dappled Things,* and most recently as the third-place winner for "Moon Dance" and honorable mention for "Intensive Care" in *2012 Tuscany Prize for Catholic Fiction – Selected Short Stories.* She says she is inspired by her Catholic faith, her family, and a deep connection to the Bible Belt South, where the conversation centers on God and sinners, family and football, and maybe a favorite old hound dog. She lives with her husband in Dothan, Alabama. The couple have five grown children and nine grandchildren, so far.

2012 TUSCANY PRIZE FOR CATHOLIC FICTION

NOVEL

Wild Spirits
By Pita Okute

NOVELLA

The Book of Jotham
By Arthur Powers

2012 Tuscany Prize for Catholic Fiction – Selected Short Stories
Edited by Joseph O'Brien

11/14